"I'd sit on a bench, you know, eating peanuts. I felt that there should be something built—some sort of an amusement enterprise—where the parents and the children could have fun together."

—Walt Disney, on watching his daughters ride a merry-go-round in Los Angeles when they were little, as he formulated his earliest ideas for Disneyland

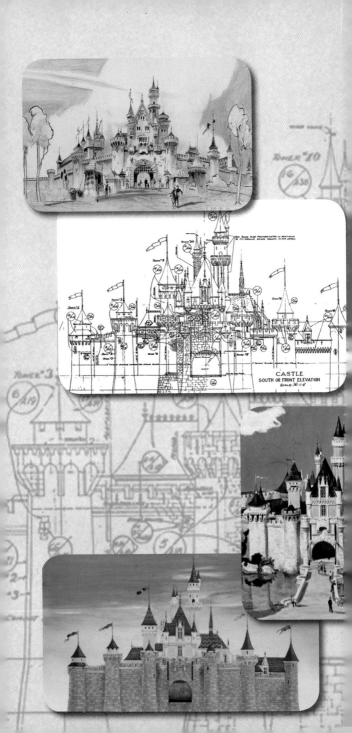

The Imagineering Field Guide to

Disneyland

An Imagineer's-Eye Tour

By The Imagineers

EDITIONS

New York

For information address Disney Editions, 1101 Flower Street, Glendale, California 91201.

Printed in Malaysia

The following are trademarks, registered marks, and service marks owned by Disney Enterprises, Inc.: Adventureland® Area, Audio-Animatronics® Figure, Big Thunder Mountain® Railroad, California Screamin', Circle-Vision, Critter Country®, Disneyland® Park, Disneyland® Resort, Disneyland® Resort Paris, Disney's Animal Kingdom® Theme Park. Disney's California Adventure® Park, Disney's Hollywood Studios™, Epcot®, Fantasyland® Area, Frontierland® Area, Imagineering, Imagineers, "it's a small world," It's Tough To Be A Bug!® Attraction, Magic Kingdom® Park, Main Street, U.S.A.® Area, Mickey's Toontown®, monorail, New Orleans Square®, Paradise Pier®, Space Mountain® Attraction, Splash Mountain® Attraction, Tomorrowland® Area, Walt Disney World® Resort

A Bug's Life, Buzz Lightyear Astro Blaster characters, Finding Nemo, and Toy Story characters © Disney Enterprises, Inc./Pixar Animation Studios

Captain EO, Indiana Jones™ Adventure and Star Tours © Disney/Lucasfilm, Ltd.

Roger Rabbit characters © Walt Disney Pictures /Amblin Entertainment, Inc.

TARZAN'S TREEHOUSE ® is a registered trademark of Edgar Rice Burroughs, Inc. All rights reserved.

The Twilight Zone® is a registered trademark of CBS, Inc., and is used pursuant to a license from CBS, Inc.

Winnie the Pooh characters based on the "Winnie the Pooh" works by A. A. Milne and E. H. Shepard.

For Disney Editions
Editorial Director: Wendy Lefkon
Senior Editor: Jody Revenson
Assistant Editor: Jessica Ward

Written and Designed by Alex Wright with help from all the Imagineers

For Everyone Who Has Ever Believed In Disneyland

The author would like to thank Jason Surrell for his ongoing support; Scott Otis for the continued use of his extensive Disney library and for his able-bodied assistance with research; Lindsay Frick for making a photo safari to catch a few extra details; Kim Irvine and Tony Baxter for a couple of fascinating walks in the Park; Jody Revenson for her continued guidance; Wendy Lefkon and Jessica Ward for all of their work behind the scenes; David Buckley for the use of his Sorcerer Mickey illustration on the cover; Denise Brown for always being there to answer an image question; Marty Sklar, Tom Fitzgerald, and Bruce Vaughn for their input and for letting him do another one of these; Jim Clark and Steve Cook for keeping everybody informed; Dave Smith and Robert Tieman for yet another thorough review; Kim, Finn, and Lincoln for giving Daddy the time to work on his book; and all Imagineers past and present for their assistance and for all the inspiration they've provided through the years.

Library of Congress Cataloging-in-Publication Data on file.

ISBN 978–14231-0975-4

First Edition

10 9 8 7 6 5

H106-9333-5-15063

TABLE OF CONTENTS

Walt Disney in front of his beloved Sleeping Beauty Castle

The Ultimate Workshop

Walt Disney Imagineering (WDI) is the design and development arm of The Walt Disney Company. "Imagineering" is Walt Disney's combination of the words *imagination* and *engineering*, highlighting the assortment of skills embodied by the group. Imagineers are responsible for master planning, designing, and building Disney parks, resorts, cruise ships, and other entertainment venues. WDI is a highly creative organization, with a broad range of skills and talents represented. Disciplines range from writers to architects, artists to engineers, and cover all the bases in between. Imagineers are playful, dedicated, and abundantly curious.

Walt was our first Imagineer, but as soon as he began developing the early ideas for Disneyland, he started recruiting others to help him realize his dream. He snapped up several of his most trusted and versatile animators and art directors to apply the skills of filmmaking to the three-dimensional world. They approached this task much the same as they would a film project. They wrote stories, drew storyboards, created inspirational art, assigned production tasks to the various film-based disciplines, and built the whole thing from scratch. Disneyland is essentially a movie that allows you to walk right in and join in the fun. As Imagineer par excellence John Hench was fond of saying in response to recent trends, "Virtual reality is nothing new . . . we've been doing that for more than fifty years!"

WDI was founded on December 16, 1952, under the name WED Enterprises (from the initials **W**alter **E**lias **D**isney). Imagineering has been an integral part of the company's culture ever since. Imagineers are the ones who ask the "what ifs?" and "why nots?" that lead to some of our most visible and most beloved landmarks. Collectively, the Disney parks have become the physical embodiment of all that our company's mythologies represent to kids of all ages.

The Dreaming Continues

Today's Imagineering is a vast and varied group, involved in projects all over the world in every stage of development, from initial conception right through to installation, and even beyond that into support and constant improvement efforts. In addition to our headquarters in Glendale, California, near the company's Burbank studios, Imagineers are based at field locations around the world. Additionally, WDI serves as a creative resource for the entire Walt Disney Company, bringing new ideas and new technologies to all of our storytellers.

Okay, Here's the Résumé

To date, Imagineers have built eleven Disney theme parks, a town, two cruise ships, dozens of resort hotels, water parks, shopping centers, sports complexes, and various entertainment venues worldwide. Some specific highlights include:

- Disneyland (1955)
- Magic Kingdom Park (1971)
- *Epcot* ® (1982)
- Tokyo Disneyland (1983)
- Disney's Hollywood Studios (1989)
- Typhoon Lagoon (1989)
- Pleasure Island (1989)
- Disneyland Resort Paris (1992)
- Town of Celebration (1994)

- Blizzard Beach (1995)
- Disney's Animal Kingdom Park (1998)
- DisneyQuest (1998)
- Disney Cruise Line (*Magic,* 1998; *Wonder,* 1999)
- ABC Times Square Studios (2000)
- Disney's California Adventure Park (2001)
- Tokyo DisneySea (2001)
- Walt Disney Studios Park Paris (2002)
- Hong Kong Disneyland (2005)

He's on Our Name Tags

The red-robed Mickey Mouse with the blue hat, who is typically used to represent WDI, is taken from his Sorcerer's Apprentice character in the classic 1940 Disney film *Fantasia.* Sorcerer Mickey is symbolic of WDI's traditional position as the loyal group of magic makers at the hand of Walt Disney, the ultimate wizard. It's worth noting that the sorcerer in *Fantasia* was named Yen Sid, or the name "Disney" spelled backward.

ALEX

WDI Disciplines

Imagineers form a diverse organization, with over 140 different job titles working toward the common goal of telling great stories and creating great places. WDI has a broad collection of disciplines considering its size, due to the highly specialized nature of our work. In everything it does, WDI is supported by many other divisions of The Walt Disney Company.

Tiki Room concept by Herb Ryman

Show/Concept Design and Illustration produces the early drawings and renderings that serve as the inspiration for our projects, and provides the initial concepts and visual communication. This artwork gives the entire team a shared vision.

Show Writing develops the stories we want to tell in the parks, as well as any nomenclature that is required. This group writes the scripts for our attractions, the copy for plaques, and names our lands, rides, shops, vehicles, and restaurants.

Architecture turns all of those fanciful show drawings into real buildings, meeting all of the functional requirements that are expected of them. Our parks and resorts present some unique architectural challenges.

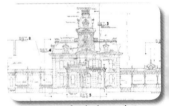

Main Street facade elevation by Larrecan

Interior dressing in Pooh Corner

Interior Designers are responsible for the design details on the inside of our buildings. They develop the look and feel of interior spaces, and select finishes, furniture, and fixtures to complete the design.

Engineering disciplines at WDI set our mechanical, electrical, and other standards and make all of our ideas work. Engineers design structures and systems for our buildings, bridges, ride systems, and play spaces, and solve the tricky problems we throw their way every day.

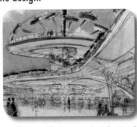

Tomorrowland concept by John Hench

Lighting Design puts all the hard work the rest of us have done on our shows and attractions into the best light. Lighting designers are also responsible for specifying all of the themed lighting fixtures found in the parks. As our lighting designers are fond of telling us, "without lights, it's radio!"

Orbiting Astro Orbitors

Graphic Designers produce signage, both flat and dimensional, in addition to providing lots of the artwork, patterns, and details that finish the Disney show. Marquees and directional signs are just a couple of examples of their work.

Monorail marquee

Prop Design is concerned with who "lives" in a given area of a park or resort. All of the pieces and parts of everyday life that tell you about a person, a time, or a place are very carefully selected and placed. These props have to be found, purchased, prepped, built, and installed.

Frontierland cannon

Sound Designers work to develop the auditory backdrop for everything you see and experience. The songs in the attractions, the background music in each of the lands, and the sound effects built into show elements all work together to complete our illusions. Sound is one of the most evocative senses.

The sweet songs of the Enchanted Tiki Room

Media Design creates all of the various film, video, audio, and on-screen interactive content in our parks. Theme Park Productions, Inc. (TPP), a sister company to WDI, serves as something of an in-house production studio.

Star Tours Storyboard by Gil Keppler

9

Landscape Architecture is the discipline that focuses on our tree and plant palette and area development. This includes the layout of all of our hardscape as well as the arrangement of the foliage elements in our lands and attractions.

Show Set Design takes concepts and breaks them down into bite-size pieces that are organized into drawing and drafting packages, integrated into the architectural, mechanical, civil, or other components of the project, and tracked during fabrication.

Show set design by Chris Smith

Character Paint creates the reproductions of various materials, finishes, and states of aging whenever we need to make something new look old.

Character Plaster produces the hard finishes in the Park that mimic other materials. This includes rock work, themed paving, and architectural facades such as faux stone and plaster. They even use concrete to imitate wood!

Dimensional Design is the art of model-making and sculpture. This skill is used to work out design issues ahead of time in model form, ensuring that our relative scales and spatial relationships are properly coordinated. Models are a wonderful tool for problem-solving.

"it's a small world" hippo by Blaine Gibson

Fabrication Design involves developing and implementing the production strategies that allow us to build all the specialized items on the large and complex projects that we deliver. Somebody has to figure out how to build the impossible!

Special Effects creates all of the magical (but totally believable) smoke, fire, water, lightning, ghosts, explosions, pixie dust, wind, rainfall, snow, and other mechanical tricks that give our stories action and a sense of surprise. Some of these effects are quite simple, while others rely on the most sophisticated technologies drawn from the field of entertainment or any other imaginable industry.

Someone had to train those piranha to attack your boat!

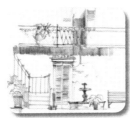

Production details by Herb Ryman

Production Design starts with the show design, takes it to the next level of detail, and ensures that it can be built so as to maintain the creative intent. It also has the task of integrating the show with all the other systems that will need to be coordinated in the field during installation.

Master Planning looks into the future and maps out the best locations and layouts for a park or a whole property. In fact, they see further into the future than any other Imagineering division, often planning locations for projects that might be many years away from realization.

Disneyland Master Plan by Marvin Davis

R&D stands for Research & Development. WDI R&D is the group that gets to play with the coolest toys. They investigate all the latest technologies from every field of study and look for ways to apply them to Disney entertainment, often inventing new ways to utilize those developments. R&D serves as a resource for the entire company.

Project Management is responsible for organizing our teams, schedules, and processes so that our projects can be delivered when they're supposed to be, within a financial framework, on schedule, and at the expected level of quality.

Construction Management ensures that every job meets Disney construction standards, including quality control, code compliance, and long-term durability during operation.

Imagineering Lingo

WDI has a very vibrant and unique culture, which is even embodied in the terms we throw around the office when we're working. Here is a guide to help you understand us a bit better as we show you around the Park.

Area Development - The interstitial spaces between the attractions, restaurants, and shops. This includes landscape architecture, propping, show elements, and special enhancements intended to expand the experience.

Audio-Animatronics - The term for the three-dimensional animated human and animal characters we employ to perform in our shows and attractions. Audio-Animatronics was invented by Imagineers at Walt's request and is an essential component of many iconic Disney attractions.

Berm - A raised earthen barrier, typically heavily landscaped, which serves to eliminate visual intrusions into the Park from the outside world and block the outside world from intruding inside.

BGM - Background Music. The musical selections that fill in the audio landscape as you make your way around the Park. Each BGM track is carefully selected, arranged, and recorded to enhance the story being told, or the area you have entered.

Blue Sky - The early stages in the idea-generation process when anything is possible. There are not yet any considerations taken into account that might rein in the creative process. At this point, the sky's the limit!

Brainstorm - A gathering for the purpose of generating as many ideas as possible in the shortest time possible. We hold many brainstorming sessions at WDI, always looking for the best ideas. Imagineering has a set of Brainstorming Rules, which are always adhered to.

> **Rule 1** - There is no such thing as a bad idea. We never know how one idea (however far-fetched) might lead into another one that is exactly right.
> **Rule 2** - We don't talk yet about *why not*. There will be plenty of time for realities later, so we don't want them to get in the way of the good ideas now.
> **Rule 3** - Nothing should stifle the flow of ideas. No buts or can'ts or other "stopping" words. We want to hear words such as "and," "or," and "what if?"
> **Rule 4** - There is no such thing as a bad idea. (We take that one very seriously.)

Charrette - Another term for a brainstorming session. From the French word for "cart." It refers to the cart sent through the Latin Quarter in Paris to collect the art and design projects of students at the legendary École des Beaux-Arts who were unable to deliver them to the school themselves after the mad rush to complete their work at the end of the term.

Concept - An idea and the effort put into communicating it and developing it into something usable. A concept can be expressed as a drawing, a written description, or simply a verbal pitch. Everything we do starts out as a concept.

Dark Ride - A term often used to describe the charming Fantasyland attractions, among others, housed more or less completely inside a show building, which allows for greater isolation of show elements and light control, as needed.

Elevation - A drawing of a true frontal view of an object—usually a building—often drawn from multiple sides, eliminating the perspective that you would see in the real world, for clarity in the design and to lead construction activities.

E-Ticket - The top level of attractions. This dates back to an early Disneyland ticketing system used to distribute ridership through all attractions in the Park. Each was assigned a letter (A,B,C,D,E) indicating where it fell in the Park's pecking order.

Kinetics - Movement and motion in a scene that give it life and energy. This can come from moving vehicles, active signage, changes in the lighting, special effects, or even hanging banners or flags that move around as the wind blows.

Maquette - A model, especially a sculpture, depicting a show element in miniature scale so that design issues can be worked out before construction begins. It's much easier to make changes on a maquette than on a full-size anything.

Plan - A direct overhead view of an object or a space. Very useful in verifying relative sizes of elements and the flow of Guests and show elements through an area.

Plussing - A word derived from Walt's penchant for always trying to make an idea better. Imagineers are continually trying to *plus* their work, even after it's "finished."

POV - Point Of View. The position from which something is seen, or the place an artist chooses to use as the vantage point of the imaginary viewer in a concept illustration. POVs are chosen in order to best represent the idea being shown.

Propping - The placement of objects around a scene. From books on a shelf to place settings on a table to wall hangings in an office space, props are the elements that give a set life and describe the people who live there. They are the everyday objects we see all around but that point out so much about our story if you pay attention to them.

Section - A drawing that looks as if it's a slice through an object or space. This is very helpful in seeing how various elements interrelate. It is typically drawn as though it were an elevation, with heavier line weights defining where our imaginary cut would be.

Show - Everything we put "onstage" in a Disney park. Walt believed that everything we put out for the Guests in our parks was part of a big show, so much of our terminology originated in the show business world. With that in mind, *show* becomes for us a very broad term that includes just about anything our Guests see, hear, smell, or come in contact with during their visit to any of our parks or resorts.

Story - Story is the fundamental building block of everything WDI does. Imagineers are, above all, storytellers. The time, place, characters, and plot points that give our work meaning start with the story, which is also the framework that guides all design decisions.

Storyboard - A large pin-up board used to post ideas in a charrette or to outline the story points of a ride or film. The technique was perfected by Walt in the early days of his animation studio and became a staple of the animated film development process. The practice naturally transferred over to WDI when so many of the early Imagineers came over from Walt's Animation department.

Theme - The fundamental nature of a story in terms of what it means to us, or the choice of time, place, and decor applied to an area in order to support that story.

THRC - Theoretical Hourly Ride Capacity. The number of guests per hour that can experience an attraction under optimal conditions. THRC is always taken into account when a new attraction is under consideration.

Visual Intrusion - Any outside element that makes its way into a scene, breaks the visual continuity, and destroys the illusion. WDI works hard to eliminate visual intrusions.

Wienie - Walt's playful term for a visual element that could be used to draw people into and around a space. A wienie is big enough to be seen from a distance and interesting enough to make you want to take a closer look, like Sleeping Beauty Castle at the end of Main Street, U.S.A. Wienies are critical to our efforts at laying out a sequence of experiences in an organized fashion.

Disneyland remains the embodiment of Walt Disney's greatest dreams. Here you are taken into realms of the past, the future, and fantasy. A day in Disneyland is a mix of nostalgia, adventure, and anticipation for what's to come. Disneyland is a playground for the child in all of us.

Aerial view of Disneyland by Peter Ellenshaw

Daddy's Day

There's a famous story Walt Disney told about going to a neighborhood park with his daughters on Saturday afternoons—Daddy's Day—and how he felt that there wasn't any place around that would allow him and the girls to have fun doing the same activities together. He sat on the bench next to the merry-go-round in Griffith Park near his studio in Burbank, eating peanuts while Diane and Sharon rode around and around. It was this experience, and all the time he had to think while sitting on that bench, that eventually led to what we know as Disneyland. These thoughts meandered along many paths before arriving at a park with the types of activities families could share in the location that we know today. His plans started out *relatively* small, but like many of Walt's ideas, they grew and grew and grew—and continue to grow even now.

The first "Disneyland" plan was drawn up for a site near the Walt Disney Studios in Burbank. It was an undeveloped plot across Riverside Drive which would one day become home to a notable building housing Walt Disney Feature Animation. This "Mickey Mouse Park" plan relied heavily on various means of transportation—trains, stagecoaches, and boats—to carry visitors through scenes and vignettes inspired by movies.

Eventually these plans gave way to an even grander vision that required much more land (eighty-plus acres, as opposed to the sixteen acres available across Riverside Drive), leading Walt to a location in Orange County—a thirty-seven mile drive from the Studio. This new concept came to define the "theme park," taking its cues from all the genres of storytelling Walt was so taken by. Walt previewed the concepts and construction of Disneyland on his weekly television show, *Disneyland*, in the year leading up to the Park's opening. Each of the proposed lands became home to a particular genre of story—encompassing adventure, fantasy, the past, and the future.

The facade of the train station welcomes you in this elevation by Marvin Davis.

Who's Your Buddy?

Even before he developed the concepts that led to Disneyland, Walt had in mind another type of show that he intended to take on the road. Walt's hobby of the late 1940s was working with miniatures. He found it very relaxing to build little scenes like those depicted in some of his films. These scenes, celebrating the sort of nostalgia and Americana Walt reveled in, were to form the basis of a traveling show, known at the time as Disneylandia. Soon his visions for these miniature scenes and the show he wanted to build around them became more and more complicated, and he started enlisting the talents of some of his mechanical wizards from the studio shops—future Imagineers Roger Broggie and Wathel Rogers, in particular—to help him flesh these scenes out to tell the stories he wanted to tell.

He started adding animation to the scenes—simple cam-driven movements that were the precursor of the later Audio-Animatronics figures. The first and most famous example of this is the Dancing Man figure seen below. This miniature performer, modeled after reference film footage of real-world entertainer Buddy Ebsen, plied his craft on a little Vaudeville proscenium stage. But before the Dancing Man was able to take his first bow, Walt was already on to a bigger and better type of Disney show.

Concept by Ken Anderson for the Dancing Man

You Oughta Be in Pictures

Disneyland concept by Herb Ryman

The Disney parks are the places where all of our favorite Disney stories come to life. At the parks we can spend time with our favorite friends and explore with them the worlds that they inhabit. Nowhere is this more true than in Disneyland, the original Disney theme park and progenitor of all that the Disney parks have become.

It has been said that Walt Disney built Disneyland "because he wanted one." It spotlights his favorite things and represents the type of world that first existed in his imagination. And the dream was clearly not his alone, for Walt was supremely in touch with the tastes and interests of his audience. When Disneyland opened in 1955, it was every child's dream to romp through Wonderland with Alice, scout Frontierland with Davy Crockett, or explore the farthest reaches of the newest frontier of outer space. Walt seized upon these dreams to create Disneyland and bring the realms of his films to life in three dimensions, allowing Guests to participate in these stories by exploring the Park at their leisure.

The Parks play a vital role in making the magic of Disney real for people all around the world. The ability to inhabit real versions of these places during a visit to Disneyland adds to the experience of viewing the films, just as knowledge of the films adds richness and depth to a day at the Park. It envelops us in these stories in a way that a two-dimensional film really can't. We can make our own way, choosing our own path, writing our own stories.

Generations of Guests have grown up in Disneyland over the course of the Park's first five decades. They've seen it change over the years. They've gone there for "Date Night." They've shared it with their kids. They've danced in Plaza Gardens. They feel that it's their Park. It is connected to Southern California and has become an important part of its history.

Does It Have to Be a Lightbulb?

That's the punch line to a commonly heard joke regarding the way Imagineers think. It starts off with the typical question, "How many (Imagineers) does it take to screw in a lightbulb?" The response offers insight into the way Imagineers like to tackle a problem—from all sides, with no stone left unturned, and challenging *all* assumptions. It's what lends us the ability to pursue the impossible dreams that make up a park like Disneyland.

From the group's inception, Imagineers have tended to defy classification. Are they artists? Engineers? Architects? Designers, writers, sculptors, business people, animators, developers? Yes. Any and all of the above—and then some. Many of these categories can find themselves intertwined on the same Imagineer's résumé. That's the nature of the work we do. The things we build are highly complex, and our process is highly collaborative. At the heart of it all, though, Imagineering is made up of both dreamers and doers. We need people who can dream those impossible dreams along with people who believe that anything is possible.

Walt's earliest Imagineers were drawn largely from the ranks of his Studio personnel, but only after it became clear to him that outside workers wouldn't be able to do what he needed to pull off the feat of translating the worlds of his films into three dimensions. Walt initially approached a good friend—the noted architect Welton Becket—asking for his firm's assistance in carrying out this vision. As Becket reviewed the concept, he quickly realized that he and his cadre of architects weren't truly suited for this kind of work. They didn't understand the timing of filmmaking, the theatrical techniques used to fool the camera (or the eye), the liberties taken with scale in the service of storytelling, or any of a number of skills and techniques that Walt already harbored within the crew on his Studio lot. From this conversation, Imagineering was born.

We are often asked the best way to get into Imagineering. There is no single answer to that question. There is no formula regarding what school to attend or what course of study to pursue. It differs for each of the 140-plus disciplines within WDI. It differs by individual. We are not all engineers. We are not all artists. But we are all storytellers and share a common sensibility regarding the value of stories. The most important thing for a future Imagineer to remember is that in the end, being an Imagineer has less to do with a specific skill set and more to do with a state of mind.

The More Things Change, The More They Change

Walt Disney once said, "Disneyland will never be completed. It will continue to grow as long as there is imagination left in the world." Walt started plussing Disneyland practically as soon as it opened and accelerated the pace of change as the Park generated more money to work with. Even after more than five decades of constant attention from the Imagineers, Disneyland is clearly not "completed."

The Park has evolved continually, through all periods of its history, and continues to do so. The Imagineers are perched just up the freeway in Glendale, constantly planning and dreaming about what they can do to the Park. On Walt's orders, the early Imagineers traveled to the Park frequently, observing the Guests and looking for ways to improve the experience in any way they could. Spending time in Disneyland is still the best way to understand what the Guests are enjoying and to discover where the opportunities to plus the Park might lie.

This evolution is what keeps Disneyland fresh. There are always new stories to tell and new Guests to tell them to. As films are generated by the Walt Disney Studios, Pixar, or any other creative entity within the company, we review them for potential application within Disneyland or any other Disney park. Those that seem promising are developed, though sometimes in different ways for different venues. We explore the best application of a given animated film for each of our parks worldwide and see which concept offers the greatest potential for an exceptional Guest experience.

Once we have our concepts ready, there is still much to be resolved before an attraction makes its way into any of our parks. There must be a consensus from all the different entities that oversee the parks to ensure that an idea is going to meet all the needs of a particular site. Many elements must align before such an important decision is made.

QUICK TAKES

- The shortest-lived attraction in Disneyland was the Mickey Mouse Club Circus—forty-six days in operation in 1955-1956.

- Fifteen attractions have remained in Disneyland since Opening Day.

- The building that has played host to the greatest number of individual attractions is the Opera House. Previous shows have included Babes in Toyland, Mickey Mouse Club Headquarters, The Walt Disney Story, and Great Moments with Mr. Lincoln.

Gone But Not Forgotten

Below is a partial list of fondly remembered attractions—all part of the ongoing history and development of Disneyland as we know it today.

Main Street, U.S.A.

- Babes in Toyland Exhibit
- Electric Cars
- The Legacy of Walt Disney
- Main Street Shooting Gallery
- Mickey Mouse Club Headquarters

Frontierland

- Conestoga Wagons
- Indian Village
- Mike Fink Keelboats
- Mine Train Through Nature's Wonderland
- Mule Pack/Pack Mules
- Rainbow Caverns Mine Train
- Rainbow Mountain Stage Coaches

Critter Country

- Country Bear Playhouse

Fantasyland

- Mickey Mouse Club Theater
- Motor Boat Cruise
- Skull Rock Cove
- Skyway between Fantasyland and Tomorrowland
- Videopolis

Tomorrowland

- Adventure Thru Inner Space
- America Sings
- Astro-Jets/Rocket Jets
- Carousel of Progress
- Circarama, U.S.A./Circle-Vision 360
- Flying Saucers
- Hall of Aluminum Fame & Hall of Chemistry
- House of the Future
- Magic Eye Theater, featuring *Captain Eo*
- PeopleMover
- Phantom Boats
- Rocket Rods
- Rocket to the Moon/Mission to Mars
- Space Station X-1/Satellite View of America
- Viewliner

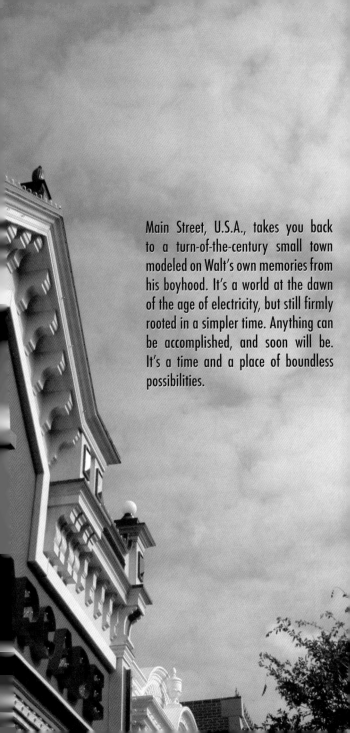

Main Street, U.S.A., takes you back to a turn-of-the-century small town modeled on Walt's own memories from his boyhood. It's a world at the dawn of the age of electricity, but still firmly rooted in a simpler time. Anything can be accomplished, and soon will be. It's a time and a place of boundless possibilities.

Main Street building block concept by Dale Hennesy

Back in the Day

Main Street, U.S.A., is the perfect way to start a day in Disneyland. It's a trip back to a time and place many Guests fondly "remember," though few of us—especially today—have actually ever been there. It is set at the dawn of the twentieth century and the advent of the widespread availability of electricity. Horseless carriages share the road with horse-drawn trolleys. Gas lamps are being replaced by electric bulbs.

Walt wanted this loving evocation of his childhood home of Marceline, Missouri to embody the American spirit. It is a place where people are friendly, hard work is rewarded, and everybody shares a dream for a better life. This is representative of Walt's heartfelt patriotism and love for his country, and is part of the message he always wanted to convey with his work.

Early Main Street concept by Harper Goff

That Hometown Feeling

In addition to Marceline, Main Street in Disneyland probably looks a lot like Ft. Collins, Colorado, the hometown of art director Harper Goff, who did many of the initial drawings of the land. This early drawing shows Harper's interpretation of those memories.

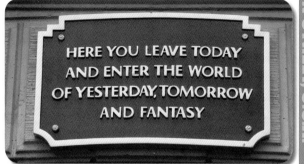

HERE YOU LEAVE TODAY AND ENTER THE WORLD OF YESTERDAY, TOMORROW AND FANTASY

The sign that welcomes you to Main Street, and to Disneyland

Reality vs Memories

Main Street, U.S.A., is based on Walt's recollections of his boyhood in Marceline, though by all accounts it is more closely tied to his *memories* of Marceline than the reality of what the town was at the time. This is an example of heightened reality, a design technique used to invoke feelings of nostalgia while taking some license with history. Heightened reality is a staple of the Imagineering toolbox, giving us the artistic license to play more directly to our Guest's emotional attachments to certain memories and design details rather than maintaining a strict adherence to absolute authenticity in those details.

Heightened reality can be observed elsewhere in the Park. The Western locale of Frontierland is an idealized version of real pioneer towns. Adventureland is a romanticized expression of the tropical locales it represents. Tomorrowland is a fantastical vision of a world of the future that probably will never exist in exactly that form. And Fantasyland combines hints of real-world architecture with exaggerated details, then heaps on excess levels of charm to depict the Medieval carnival, the Alpine village, and the English Tudor style we've always imagined in our storybooks. All of these examples rely on the same formula—take the things people "know" from the world around them, select the ones that suit the story you wish to tell, and combine them into something that is entirely new but that still feels oddly familiar.

Main Street facade elevations by Kim Irvine

Ridin' the Rails

Walt working on the Lilly Belle *at his Holmby Hills home*

You can't properly tell the story of Disneyland without talking about trains. Walt's love of trains, and the shared fascination he found with several of his animators at the Studio, forms one of the essential building blocks of Walt's parks. He built a miniature line—the Carolwood Pacific—in his backyard as a hobby. All of the early iterations of what would become Disneyland, including some initial plans for the little Riverside park at the Walt Disney Studios, prominently featured a train as a means of providing transportation, setting the scene, and telling the story. Originally known as the Santa Fe and Disneyland Railroad, this line has been a fixture of the Park since Opening Day, and remains one of its most recognizable landmarks. The berm upon which it rides serves as the Park boundary and visual intrusion barrier for much of its perimeter. This idea grew out of his backyard layout, where he had placed an earthen barrier around his property so as not to bother the neighbors with the noise from his train!

Making Tracks . . . The various routes to Disneyland taken by each engine

• Engine No. 1, the *C.K. Holliday*—Built at the Studio and patterned after the *Lilly Belle* of the Carolwood Pacific Railroad, this engine was named after the founder of the Santa Fe railroad.

• Engine No. 2, the *E.P. Ripley*—Built alongside the *C.K. Holliday* and named after one of Santa Fe's early presidents.

• Engine No. 3, the *Fred G. Gurley*—The first locomotive not built by the Studio, this one was manufactured in 1894 by Baldwin Locomotives, and spent most of its life in Louisiana. It is named after the chairman of the Santa Fe Railroad in 1958, at the time it entered service in Disneyland.

• Engine No. 4, the *Ernest S. Marsh*—Added a year later in 1959, this engine is a 1925 Baldwin locomotive found in New England and named after the then-president of the Santa Fe Railroad.

• Engine No. 5, the *Ward Kimball*—A 1902 Baldwin operating since 2005, named for one of Walt's key animators, whose fascination with trains was matched perhaps only by Walt's.

Fire Engine elevation by Bob Gurr and Sam McKim

"A" Ticket to Ride

Part of the atmosphere of any time or place is the style of the vehicles that move about. This can go a long way toward explaining to a visitor the nature of any sort of imaginary setting. Our vehicles are one of the most direct reflections of the level of technology, the density of a population, and the activity level. Is the city bustling? Is the town booming? Is the rural area industrialized? These questions can typically be answered with a quick glance at the local transportation systems.

Much of the charm of Main Street, U.S.A., comes from the assortment of vehicles that share the street with the pedestrians. It's the classic juxtaposition of the horseless carriage and the horse-drawn trolley that tells you instantly just what time you're in and what sort of place it is. We have the trolleys, we have the jitneys (old-fashioned automobiles of various vintages), and we have the ever-popular fire engine. When the Park used tiered ticket books for attractions, the vehicles on Main Street tended to be A-Tickets, the simplest of rides. Just having them around on the street makes for a more complete and convincing environment—one that feels lived-in and alive.

The cumulative effect of all this activity is to reinforce the notion that this is an exciting place, bristling with energy. The vehicles offer a great tour of Main Street, as well as a chance to rest your feet and get a lift from here to there. The drivers all know this town like the back of their hand, so they're always excellent sources of information. Whether you're here for the first time or the hundred and first, these vehicles help make your visit to our little town pleasant and evocative.

QUICK TAKE

• It's been said that Walt used to come into Disneyland in the morning prior to opening so that he could drive the Carnation milk truck around Main Street.

Long, medium, and close shots of Disney Clothiers Ltd.

I'm Ready for My Close-up, Mr. D.

Main Street is one of the best places to scout examples of the WDI practice of designing for "close, medium, and long shots," articulated so well over the years by Imagineer John Hench. The idea is that long views establish an idea, medium views continue to support the idea, and close-ups provide elements that reinforce the story. This is why we pay so much attention to details such as carpet patterns, doorknobs, lighting fixtures, and furniture. If you keep the story in mind as you select these elements and coordinate well with a design approach that's been established for a given scene, it allows for a consistency of concept, eliminating anything that contradicts it.

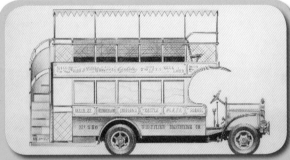

Nice Wheels

Elevation of the Main Street Omnibus by Bob Gurr

If you've ever hopped aboard a piece of Disneyland transportation to set off on another adventure, you've probably encountered the work of Bob Gurr. This designer, who joined WED straight out of the transportation design program at Art Center College of Design, set the standard for all vehicle design in Disneyland. He is responsible for the Main Street vehicles, the Matterhorn Bobsleds, the original monorail, and Casey, Jr. among others. And he insisted on driving the first example of each of his creations, if it was street-legal, from the Studio down to Disneyland himself!

MAIN STREET, U.S.A.

DISNEYLAND

We'll Leave the Light On

The lantern visible through the upstairs window of the Fire Station is a reminder of the days when Walt kept watch over the Park from up there. This family apartment, built into the original design of the Park, was his home away from home. He left a lamp on in the window to let the Cast Members know when he was staying over.

Spare No Expense

Even as funding was running low during the construction of the Park, Walt insisted on furnishing Disneyland with only the finest fixtures and finishes. He felt that the ambience created by such quality would add to the perception of value.

QUICK TAKES

• The Hub and Spoke plan system that defines the Park's layout is a key to the ease with which Guests navigate from land to land.

• Walt wanted the storefront windows on Main Street to be placed closer to the ground than would be period-correct so that children would be able to see inside.

• The bright red of the sidewalks in Town Square and in the Hub area in front of the castle was chosen to enhance the green of the grass, as the two colors are opposites on the color wheel.

• The music is, of course, chosen to represent the period, but also to evoke a sense of optimism with its fanfare of upbeat, bouncy tempos.

• Many of the windows over Main Street are lit from behind with flicker lamps, and some even have special effects that cast shadows to make the buildings continue to feel occupied after dark.

• The Main Street Opera House was the first building completed in Disneyland, when Admiral Joe Fowler, in charge of the Park's construction, concluded that he needed a place to house an on-site mill in order to get all the required woodwork done in time to meet the Park's opening day deadline.

Walt's father is remembered on this window.

A Window to the Past

One of the most treasured traditions within the Walt Disney Company is the honor of having one's name placed on a window on Main Street. The windows serve as a fascinating look into the backgrounds of the people who have made the magic happen. The folks represented on these windows come from many different areas of the Company. There are Imagineers, operators, developers, corporate officers, artisans, and more. The common thread is that they are all credited with making a significant impact on the Magic Kingdom and the legacy of Disney parks.

Each window is carefully designed, the way any other element in the Park would be. The imaginary profession of the new resident of Main Street is typically chosen to relate to the activities or personal interests of the real-world counterpart. Some of the cleverest turns of a phrase in all of Disney Park nomenclature can be found here. The graphic layout is handled by one of our designers, and nowadays the honoree receives a scale-model replica at a ceremony held on Main Street at which the real window is revealed.

Window Stopping

Here's a guide for some of the Imagineering names you might see on Main Street that you may or may not have heard of:

• Ken Anderson, an animation art director, was a key figure in establishing the Imagineering language used to transfer our fantasy film environments into the real, built spaces of Disneyland.

• Marvin Davis worked with Walt to create the earliest layouts of Disneyland, when it moved from the Studio site and the scope of the project grew tremendously. It is through these efforts that the famous Hub and Spoke layout of the Park was devised.

• Claude Coats was one of the early Imagineers to come over from the Studio. He was an accomplished background artist who led the creation of some of the most amazing environments Imagineering has ever created, including Pirates of the Caribbean and The Haunted Mansion.

• Don DaGradi was one of the top story artists at the Studio—having worked on films such as *Pinocchio*, *Fantasia*, *Peter Pan*, *Sleeping Beauty*, and *Mary Poppins*—and worked on Disneyland in its early days.

• Blaine Gibson was an animator at the Studio until Walt brought him over to WED and decided that he'd make a good sculptor. He turned out to be WED's master sculptor and established the Imagineering approach to sculpture for theme-park attractions. Blaine sculpted the Partners statue of Walt and Mickey found in the Hub.

• Richard Irvine was a Hollywood art director who played a lead role in the development of Disneyland and Walt Disney World. One of WED's first employees, he eventually became head of all design.

• Fred Joerger was one of the three original members of the WED model shop. He had worked as a model-builder for the Studio, developing miniatures used to design sets or to be used on film.

• Emile Kuri, former head of the Studio set-decorating department, designed many of the Park's interior spaces and also served as Walt's personal decorator. He decorated Walt's family apartment over the Fire Station on Main Street, U.S.A.

• Wathel Rogers, another Disney animator who found his way over to WED at Walt's suggestion, was instrumental in the development of Audio-Animatronics technology. Walt had previously taken note of Wathel's hobbies of sculpture and mechanical design, and put him to work in the Studio prop shop.

ADVENTURELAND

Adventureland re-creates the eras and locales of great adventure stories. To Walt, it was a "wonder land of nature's own design." Here you'll navigate the tropical rivers of the world, explore Indian temple ruins, and climb into the tree canopy in the deepest jungles of Africa. Adventureland is for the young at heart and brave of spirit.

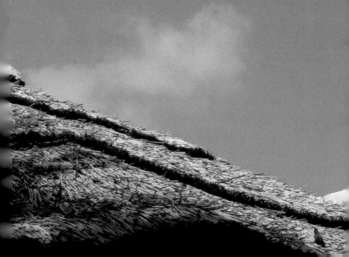

A whole world of adventure beckons you in this concept by Sam McKim.

What Does "Adventure" Look Like?

It's a good question, isn't it? *Adventure* is a very broad term that brings to mind a very broad range of images. For some, it can be a time, for others a place. For others still, it has more to do with a spirit or a state of mind. So, how do you create a place that looks like adventure to *everyone*? Figuring that out was one of the first tasks assigned by Walt to his Imagineers.

Since many disparate images come to mind when one hears the word "adventure," our Adventureland intentionally plays on several of these themes and settings. There are the deep, dark jungles of Africa; the South Seas tropics; and a tropical bazaar. It is the combination of all the locales within that creates an overall sense of adventure to serve as a backdrop for the stories we want to tell.

The *Disneyland* television show, which served as Walt's introduction of the Park to his future Guests, began each segment with a brief introduction that linked that evening's presentation to one of the lands he had planned for Disneyland, and many offered a progress report on the Park under construction. The stories on which the Park was based in the first place were now put to use to explain the new Park to others. There were Davy Crockett episodes for Frontierland, tales of space travel for Tomorrowland, and animated stories for Fantasyland. These, along with the True-Life Adventure series of documentary films, served notice as to what Walt had in mind for his Park and with this land. As a matter of fact, in the early planning stages for Disneyland, Adventureland was referred to by the working title True-Life Adventureland.

Jungle Cruise elevation by Harper Goff

Ready, Set, Design!

Harper Goff, one of the first Imagineers brought on board by Walt—straight from his work on the Disney film *20,000 Leagues Under the Sea*—left his stamp all over Disneyland. His designs were particularly influential in the flavor and charm of Main Street, U.S.A., and in the character and mystery of Adventureland. His broad experience as a motion picture art director made him a perfect choice to render and produce Walt's ambitious visions in three dimensions.

QUICK TAKES

• Harper Goff finalized details of the layout of the signature feature of Adventureland—the exotic environment of Jungle Cruise—on-site by using a sandbox that simulated the attraction footprint. Harper used his foot to sculpt the sand into the shapes of the river and its banks, locating landmarks along the way; then workers would replicate these forms using their bulldozers and shovels.

• Prior to the land's opening, orange trees from the site were uprooted and replanted upside down with bromeliads on top—the former roots—by master landscaper Bill Evans to simulate the exotic plant life of these remote and mostly unknown environs, when the real plant material was either not available or was not viable in this location.

Tiki Room entry concept by Herb Ryman and John Hench

Jungle Cruise concept by Harper Goff

Animal Adventures

Jungle Cruise was one of the first attractions not based on a Disney animated film. On the suggestion of Harper Goff, the attraction took its inspiration from a popular movie of the 1950s featuring a journey through a jungle by boat. Walt's early plans for Jungle Cruise included real, live animals. Inspired by the success of his True-Life Adventure films, he was determined to bring these wonders of nature to a place where Guests could see them up close and share his admiration. Upon consultation with animal-care specialists, Walt realized that although the domesticated mules and horses in Frontierland could generally be counted on to perform their roles, live exotic animals would not provide the consistent show he wanted. They couldn't be trusted to stay in areas in which they'd remain visible, they'd sleep most of the day, and they'd surely be irritated by the constant boatloads of gawkers and the special effects required to tell the story. The parks would not get their exotic animal experiences until many years later, upon the opening of Disney's Animal Kingdom Theme Park at Walt Disney World in 1998, when clever, new design techniques enabled separation of animals from the people viewing them.

Jungle Cruise set a new precedent for humor in Disneyland. In 1962, when Walt first brought master animator Marc Davis over to WED to try his hand at designing for Disneyland, he asked Marc to take a trip to check out the Park. He wanted to hear Marc's impressions of the place. Marc's first comment was that there was nothing funny there. He thought the Park needed some gags, and Jungle Cruise was one of his first and most recognizable efforts.

Jungle Cruise boat elevation by Harper Goff

Distress Signaled

In preparation for the 1993 arrival of the Indiana Jones™ Adventure next door, the Jungle Cruise boats underwent a makeover to shift their design toward this new, more gritty, and realistic aesthetic that was being introduced to Adventureland. They lost the red and white striped canopies, gained some adventurous propping, and had scenic paint treatments applied to add years of age and use to their hulls.

From Reality to Humor

The art of the WDI sight gag was perfected by Imagineer Marc Davis. One of Walt's Nine Old Men, he was known to be one of the finest draftsmen ever to work at the Studio. His work for Walt Disney Animation, including the classic characters Tinker Bell, Princess Aurora, and Cruella De Vil, gave him an impeccable sense of timing that allowed his creations to read instantly—an important consideration in light of the limited time and dialogue available as the audience moves through a scene. His gag sketches for Jungle Cruise were often translated practically verbatim into the attraction. His work was instrumental in the development of some of Imagineering's most beloved creations, such as Pirates of the Caribbean, The Haunted Mansion, Country Bear Jamboree, and the Carousel of Progress. His legendary conceptual work for the Western River Expedition concept for Magic Kingdom Park paved the way for Big Thunder Mountain Railroad. Marc's sense of humor has come to define the distinctive style of humor that the Disney parks are known for.

Fire pit scene concept by Bryan Jowers

If Adventureland Has a Name . . .

For those who grew up with George Lucas and Steven Spielberg's Indiana Jones™ films, there is no truer expression of the sense of adventure than the world inhabited by our favorite archaeologist. This cultural touchstone was so compelling that it led to one of our most ambitious attractions. The films even had a built-in Disneyland connection as well, as director Steven Spielberg had sent his sound designers down to the Park to record Big Thunder Mountain Railroad for the second film's mine-chase scene!

It's Going to Be a Bumpy Ride!

The enhanced motion vehicle (EMV) ride system used for the troop transports in the Indiana Jones™ Adventure was developed originally for this attraction, and is a key component of its tremendous success. The vehicle consists of a moving platform capable of stopping, going, cornering, climbing, and descending—all while carrying a hydraulic motion-base system that offers the attraction's designers the ability to program pitch, roll, and yaw movements to enhance the experience. The real benefit of a vehicle with these capabilities is that it provides new ways to create experiences for the riders, as they interact with a stunning array of moving set pieces, Audio-Animatronics characters, projections, and special effects. The vehicle can bump as it goes down a "staircase". It can get "bogged down in the mud," or swerve to evade an attack. It becomes another character in the story.

Language Skills

As Imagineers, we often create rules to govern the design and development of entire worlds, but rarely do we create an alphabet. For the Indiana Jones™ Adventure, however, concept designer Chuck Ballew did just that. Chuck devised a written language, called Maraglyphics, which decorates the queue and gives Guests another layer of story to decipher prior to boarding their troop transport.

This Herb Ryman sketch shows another direction that was pursued prior to the development of the EMV. This approach would have taken its cue primarily from Indiana Jones and the Temple of Doom. We typically look at an idea from several different directions before settling on the option we think is the best. Often, this leads us to some of our greatest advances.

At one point, the ambitious concept called for the EMV ride system, the runaway mine cart, the incorporation of the Disneyland Railroad, and even the Jungle Cruise boats converging inside a massive Indiana Jones™ show building, as seen in this amazing concept image by Bryan Jowers.

QUICK TAKE

• The Indiana Jones™ Adventure was built in a space that was formerly part of the Disneyland parking lot. The engaging queue space moves Guests out beyond and beneath the train route to the show building. The intricate detailing and the interactive elements were devised by the design team to bring the Guest into the story well before they ever board their vehicle.

Concept by Bryan Jowers

Hidden lighting fixtures

Drumming Up Business

During a 2004 rehab of Walt Disney's Enchanted Tiki Room courtyard and the Adventureland entrance, the design team came up with a clever way to integrate the necessary nighttime lighting into the ornamentation on the thatched roof adjacent to the land marquee. The lighting fixtures were hidden in South Seas drums used as an element in the rooftop decor. We often devise similar solutions for show lighting, speaker placements, and fireworks launch locations throughout the Park.

Walt Disney's Enchanted Tiki Room concept by Collin Campbell

Local Vocals

Two of the voice talents heard in Walt Disney's Enchanted Tiki Room have extensive connections to Disneyland. Wally Boag and Fulton Burley, who voice José and Michael, respectively, were longtime performers in the Golden Horseshoe Revue in Frontierland. A third singing bird, Fritz, was given song by Thurl Ravenscroft, a favorite Disney voice known for his performances in The Haunted Mansion, Country Bear Jamboree, Disneyland Railroad, and on the *Mark Twain* Riverboat. He even voices the character of Tangaroa in the Tiki Room pre-show!

QUICK TAKES

•The native encampment in Jungle Cruise is in reality only about thirty-five feet from City Hall on Main Street, U.S.A., illustrating the art of WDI illusion. It's all about sight lines and separation of spaces.

•The density of the landscaping in Adventureland also works to heighten another of the core elements of the Disneyland experience—anticipation. So much of our excitement during the course of a day here stems from our expectations of what will happen next. We're primed to expect great things, but we don't know what those might be. Nowhere is this more satisfying than in Adventureland, a place where we set off to explore the unknown with a sense that anything can happen.

Bill Evans developed our technique of planting "hero" trees such as this one.

The Seeds of Good Design

Legendary Imagineer Bill Evans came to work for Disney through his experience doing landscape design for Walt's home. Walt invited him to come out to work on a new venture he was undertaking, and Bill became one of the most influential Imagineers ever. From the earliest days of Disneyland, Bill developed the techniques that came to define the WDI approach to landscape design—a significant component of all of our parks. It was an entirely new mode of thinking that treated the landscape elements of the parks as key parts of the story—a very theatrical aesthetic. For nearly fifty years, Bill lent his green thumb to Disney parks around the world, through Disney's Animal Kingdom in 1998. Bill even contributed some show writing to the mix, when Walt asked him to put fancy Latin names on the patches of weeds in unfinished portions of the Park in the days leading up to its opening.

Tarzan's Treehouse concept by Bryan Jowers

Tip-top

Sometimes a film comes along that just begs to be brought to life in our parks. If the 1999 animated film *Tarzan* didn't belong in Adventureland, nothing did. The classic story of Tarzan made a perfect fit to bring a new story into the Park while still making use of the landmark tree that had housed the venerable Swiss Family Treehouse found here since its opening in 1962.

During the 1999 conversion to Tarzan's Treehouse, the design team added a new entryway in the middle of the path leading to New Orleans Square and Frontierland. This was done for two reasons. First, to give the attraction a greater presence and a more interesting composition. Secondly, to create a visual barrier at the end of the path to shield the view toward Pirates of the Caribbean and the Frontierland promenade, as these elements had been a bit too highly visible from almost all of Adventureland. Now we have a better reveal as you discover the paths around the tree and make the transition from land to land.

Scene concept by Steve Abernathy

Walt Disney's Enchanted Tiki Room concept by Collin Campbell

A Bird of a Different Feather

Our first Audio-Animatronics show in Disneyland in 1963, Walt Disney's Enchanted Tiki Room was often said to have been Walt's favorite. Not bad for an attraction originally conceived as a restaurant—one with a show, of course! Dinner theater concepts had been explored for Disneyland but none had ever made it to construction. After Walt returned from a trip to New Orleans with a little mechanical bird, he became fixated on the idea of improving the mechanism and building a show around singing birds. Eventually he settled on a Tiki backdrop for his singing birds, allowing him to place it in Adventureland. This choice of theming also allowed for the introduction of a huge supporting cast of flowers, masks, drummers, and tikis, all singing along in unison. The tiki motif is especially relevant in the Southern California locale of the Park, as tiki was a significant pop-culture movement in this area in the 1950s and 1960s.

In 2004, Walt Disney's Enchanted Tiki Room saw a complete and painstaking refurbishment in which the show was restored to its original condition. The team re-manufactured the internal components of each of the Audio-Animatronics figures, in addition to lots of new feathers, new artificial foliage, updated show programming, and a renovation of all of the mechanical effects in the pre-show in the forecourt garden.

Parrot maquette by Blaine Gibson

43

FRONTIERLAND

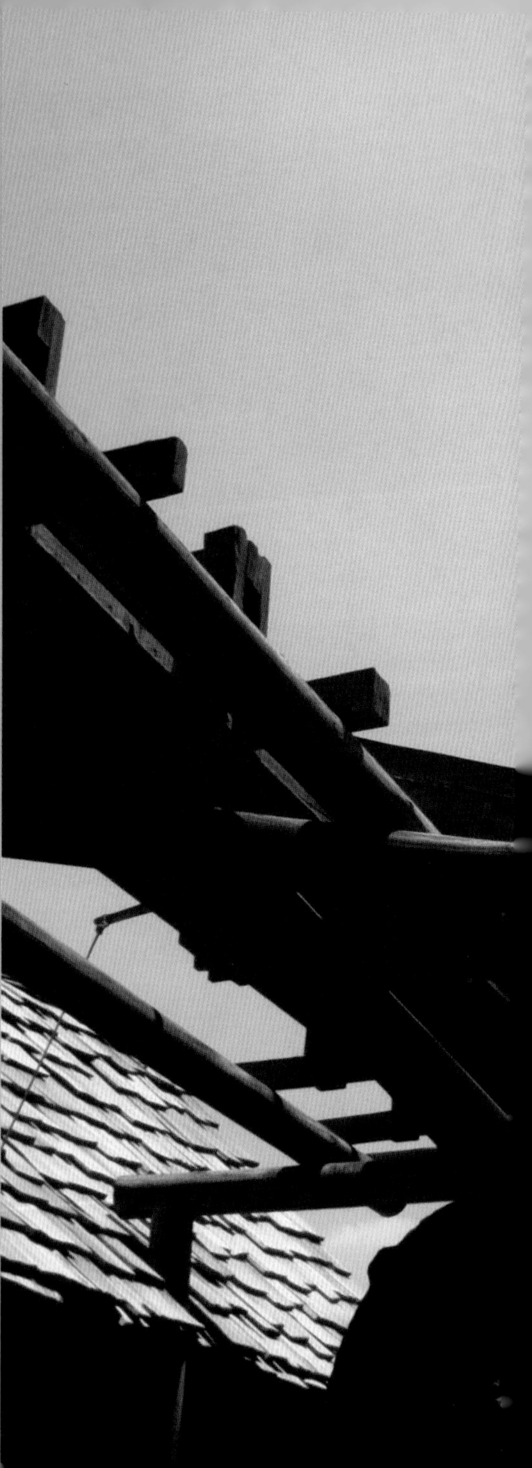

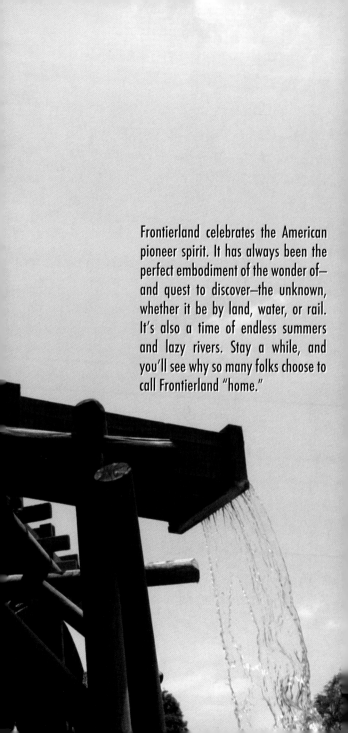

Frontierland celebrates the American pioneer spirit. It has always been the perfect embodiment of the wonder of—and quest to discover—the unknown, whether it be by land, water, or rail. It's also a time of endless summers and lazy rivers. Stay a while, and you'll see why so many folks choose to call Frontierland "home."

Frontierland overview by Herb Ryman

Go West, Young Guests!

Frontierland could be described as the most distinctly American statement in all of Disneyland. It serves as a tribute to the pioneering spirit that drove Americans westward in covered wagons and stagecoaches—a subject that was as near and dear to Walt as Main Street, U.S.A., and equally connected to the fondest memories from his childhood. It's brimming with the excitement of discovery.

The settings of Frontierland represent a time span of roughly ninety years—1790 to 1880. Like Adventureland, Frontierland is made up of several design motifs, each tied into different bits of American folklore. We see the wooded frontier of Davy Crockett; the southern banks of the mighty Mississippi, recalling the world of Tom Sawyer; the Southwestern U.S., identified with the tall tales of Pecos Bill and other American legends; and Big Thunder Mountain Railroad's abandoned ghost town, left behind after the gold rush of 1849.

Frontierland is all about the details. Raised wooden sidewalks over the streets of the town are there to keep mud and dust off the boots and dresses of the locals. Hitching posts provide the means to tie your horse in place while you mosey about. Posted graphics on the walls give us a sense of the time and place of this rustic town. The landscaping is designed to be more natural in appearance than that in the rest of Disneyland and is maintained in this less-manicured state. The plant palette makes use of a type of forced perspective to enhance the feeling of space, bringing the larger species within close proximity of our Guests and placing smaller, closer-planted varieties farther away. This Western-themed land even lies, fittingly, on the western side of our park.

Frontierland concept by Herb Ryman

A Sense of Scale

On opening day, Frontierland occupied roughly one third of the area of the Park. This was partly due to the popularity at that time of movies and television shows set in the West, but there were also design principles at work. Compared to the relatively confined passageways of Main Street, U.S.A., Fantasyland, and Adventureland, Frontierland offers expansive vistas in keeping with the sense of discovery and possibility that Walt and his Imagineers wanted to capture for this land.

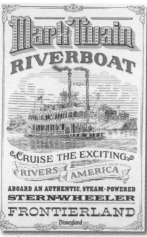

Riverboat poster by Debbie Floyd

A Graphic Explanation

The environmental, atmospheric graphics that inhabit a land go a long way toward fleshing it out and making it believable. The signs that one finds on the walls are part of everyday life, and a park environment that lacks them feels sterile and "fake." In Disneyland, we create graphic elements that assist us with our placemaking through their design and tell our backstory through their content.

Frontierland entry concept by Herb Ryman

Early concept for Big Thunder Mountain Railroad by Tony Baxter

Hats and Glasses, Beware!

The "wildest ride in the wilderness" made its debut in 1979. Big Thunder Mountain Railroad took the previously existing genre of the mine-car ride and elevated it to a different level. The planning and execution of the environment made it much more than a roller coaster. For example, rock work was designed so that it appears to have been there before the 2,671 feet of railroad track were laid, rather than to have grown up around a ride track set into place by theme-park designers. The team had to produce nine iterations of the model of the mountain in their attempts to integrate the mountain and track in this way. It was a tremendous effort, but this gave it the more naturalistic appearance that is such a big part of the attraction's charm.

The mountain rises 104 feet in the air, covers two acres of land, and is decorated with lots of authentic antique gold-digging gear—ore cars, lanterns, barrels, tools, and mining equipment such as an old ball mill used to extract gold from ore, and a double-stamp ore-crusher. The landscaping of sagebrush and pine helps to complete the setting.

Big Thunder Mountain Railroad was derived from a Western River Expedition attraction planned by Marc Davis for Magic Kingdom Park in Walt Disney World. That massive concept featured a Pirates of the Caribbean-like boat ride through scenes in the American West, along with hiking trails, pack-mule rides, and, yes, a runaway mine train, all housed in an enormous complex known as Thunder Mesa. That specific project was never realized, but the core of the idea was so strong that it had to find a home somewhere. Ironically, the attraction was built in Disneyland before Walt Disney World got its version.

A Rock Is a Rock Is a . . . Rock?

The California and Florida Big Thunder Mountains use different geographic references for their rock work. Anaheim's is based on Utah's Bryce Canyon National Park, while Orlando's is based on Monument Valley, also in Utah and Arizona, but with very distinct characteristics. Bryce Canyon is striated, heavily eroded, and magenta in color. Monument Valley is angular and rendered in earthy tones. Why was this choice made? Location, location, location. Big Thunder Mountain in Disneyland lies on the east side of the Rivers of America rather than the west, making it visible from Fantasyland. So, the colorful Bryce Canyon rock work is used to create something of a *candy mountain* backdrop.

Rock work styling for Big Thunder Mountain Railroad in a concept by Dan Goozee

UICK TAKES

• The little mining town called Big Thunder visible from the queue was once part of Rainbow Ridge, the point of departure for the earlier Mine Train Through Nature's Wonderland.

• The phosphorescent pools, springs, waterfalls, and geysers in the cave are a nod to the previous Rainbow Caverns Mine Train.

Big Thunder Mountain Range . . . Mines all mines

Disneyland Park	Magic Kingdom Park	Tokyo Disneyland	Disneyland Paris
1979	1980	1983	1992

Riverboat Reveries

Mark Twain concept by Stan Parkhouse

Often photographed as a Park icon, and serving as a wienie drawing Guests into Frontierland, the *Mark Twain* riverboat speaks volumes about the unique nature of Disneyland and the elements within it. This staple of early frontier life is re-created here, and seen in a setting in which it has not existed in the real world for decades. It offers Guests both young and old an opportunity to experience a bit of our past. Walt felt so strongly about the importance of the riverboat in Disneyland that when construction funding fell short, he paid for its completion out of his own pocket.

A voyage on the *Mark Twain* is as much about what is seen along the shore as it is about the riverboat itself. A lap around the Rivers of America gives us an overview of all of Frontierland and a glimpse into what the land is about. The Indian Village, the settler's cabin, the views of Big Thunder Mountain Railroad, and other parts of Tom Sawyer's Island all tell us about the spirit of the American frontier.

The Indian Village along the banks in a concept by Sam McKim

That Ship Has Sailed

Sailing Ship Columbia *concept by Sam McKim*

Some of the work created by Imagineers is fanciful and purely the product of imagination. On occasion, however, our stories call for us to re-create something of historical significance. In these instances, we strive to achieve the highest degree of accuracy, and put our attention toward design research and gaining an understanding of the material and fabrication technologies that would have been brought to bear at the time so that we can impart the most complete experience possible.

In the case of the Sailing Ship *Columbia*, the choice to pursue a faithful reproduction is due to the importance of the original ship upon which it is based. That vessel—built in Norwell, Massachusetts—left Boston Harbor in 1787 on a mission to "carry the Stars and Stripes around the World." It returned three years later as the first American ship to circumnavigate the globe, having sailed 41,899 nautical miles. In creating our full-scale replica, difficulty arose when it was discovered that there were no copies of the plans for the original vessel, save for a single sketch. Re-created blueprints were developed by maritime expert Ray Wallace. Under the direction of Admiral Joe Fowler, the resultant design was executed by the Todd Shipyards in Long Beach, California, and launched in Disneyland in June 1958.

UICK TAKES

• Plans for the well-known HMS *Bounty* were tracked down and used for reference on this re-creation of the *Columbia*, as the two ships were built just two years apart, possibly by many of the same shipbuilders following their emigration to the United States.

• The display belowdecks was added in 1964 as a floating museum to offer Guests a view of eighteenth-century maritime life.

The Gift That Just Keeps on Giving

For the couple's thirty-first wedding anniversary in 1956, Walt bought his wife a truly unique anniversary gift—a petrified tree stump he had purchased on a tour of the American West. As thrilled as Lilly must have been by this, she couldn't see much use for it around the house. Thinking quickly, she got the idea to donate her lovely gift to Walt's park so that all of his Guests could enjoy it in its new Frontierland home. And they have for years.

Wandering Window

One of several commemorative windows that has wandered away from Main Street, U.S.A., is that for Fess Parker, who played Davy Crockett on the Disney TV show of the 1950s. The coonskin caps referenced on the window were a nationwide phenomenon around the time the Park opened.

Bigger is Better

One day as Walt looked out at the activity on his Rivers of America with Dick Nunis, one of his key Park managers, he spoke about the selection of vessels he saw out on the water. He made note of the fact that they now had canoes, rafts, keelboats, and, of course, the mighty *Mark Twain* riverboat. He said to Dick, "Now there's a busy river." Nunis, with his focus on efficiency, assumed that Walt was about to express a desire to reduce the number of boats to ease congestion and simplify the operation. He was quite surprised when Walt said, instead, "What we need is another *big* boat." He was looking to plus the river, so the next addition to the fleet was the Sailing Ship *Columbia*. Now we have another big boat to vary the scale and make the rounds.

Happy trails in Frontierland

A Fork in the Road

When designing our parks, many considerations are made to ensure that we maintain comfortable spatial relationships between elements. In Disneyland, this adds to the charm that people experience as they make their way through the Park. But Disneyland has to accommodate large numbers of Guests, so the pathways have to be of a certain minimum width just to allow them to move about. The way we keep the comfortable pedestrian scale and the charm of the Park is by dividing the paths with planting zones and greenbelts, avoiding large, unbroken expanses of concrete. It has been said at WDI that a forty-foot-wide path may be efficient, but twenty feet twice is charming. This notion plays itself out all over the Park, from the sculpted planter gardens in Fantasyland to the mostly edible greenscape of Tomorrowland. The expanse of the Hub in front of Sleeping Beauty Castle is broken up by pockets of flowers and other landscaping, not to mention the water elements that dot the pathways and vistas of the entire Park. Through the use of these and other devices, we are able to move our Guests around without losing their connection to their surroundings.

An Illuminating Moment

These flickering cold-blast lanterns, identified by the pipes recirculating air to the top of the lamp to feed the combustion, help set the date for the land as late as 1880, when this "new" technology brought brighter, more efficient nighttime lighting.

Concept design for the Pirates Point stage show by Wesley Keil

Straight from the Source

WDI works very hard to maintain the integrity of our stories. So when the Imagineers were asked to try to find a way to bring pirates to Tom Sawyer Island—owing to the immense popularity of the films based on Pirates of the Caribbean—they feared that they would not be able to do so without contradicting the existing story lines. Soon, though, the team discovered that the worlds of pirates and Tom Sawyer were not so difficult to reconcile. A review of the history of the island showed that pirates and treasure were ideas that had already made the rounds at WED, and a review of the original literary source by Mark Twain reminded the designers that Tom and Huck had originally set out on the river to become pirates and search for treasure. Early concepts showed that piracy had been explored as a world of play for Tom and Huck. The island itself even bore hints of this pirate past—Castle Rock had been tagged "Pirates Den" by the boys since opening and Smuggler's Cove had been called Pirate's Cove through most of its development.

Concept by Chris Runco of the discovery of a pirate map

Concepts for interactive adventures by Wesley Keil

Good Ideas Never Go Away

In the Park's early days, concept art was created—some of it for marketing—that focused on the angle of playing pirate on Tom Sawyer Island. When the team found this Art Riley piece along with others by him and Sam McKim, they were reassured that they were on the right track—one that Walt had pursued years earlier.

QUICK TAKES

• Laffite's Tavern ties the island to Jean Laffite's anchor, which is located in a planter facing the Rivers of America near the raft dock. Jean Laffite spent much time in New Orleans plotting his pirate exploits. The plaque identifying the anchor warns against believing "everything you read."

• Dead Man's Grotto presents a backstory involving generations of pirates who've hidden their treasures there, only to have them pilfered by others. They're still down there digging. You just can't trust a pirate!

• Tom and Huck's tree house was a pre-existing element brought into our current story with just a re-dressing with pirate-y decor. There is a treasure map in the tree house drawn up by Tom and Huck and signed by them and their friends.

• Even the marquee at the dock has been designed to appear as though it has been taken over by pirates.

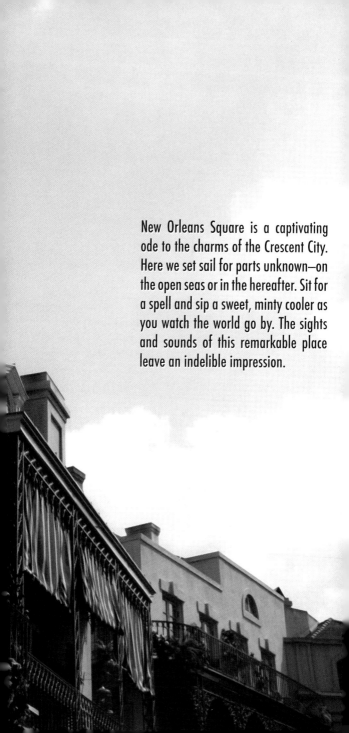

New Orleans Square is a captivating ode to the charms of the Crescent City. Here we set sail for parts unknown—on the open seas or in the hereafter. Sit for a spell and sip a sweet, minty cooler as you watch the world go by. The sights and sounds of this remarkable place leave an indelible impression.

The spirit of New Orleans is captured in this concept by Herb Ryman.

We Need Something on that Bend in the River

New Orleans Square represented a very significant expansion that forever changed the face of Disneyland. Making its debut in 1966—eleven years after the opening of the Park—this last major project overseen by Walt was the first new land added since the original five. Not only that, but it brought, in a very short span of time, two of the most distinctive attractions ever to appear in a Disney park.

Walt had always thought that this stretch of the Rivers of America, with its Mississippi stern-wheeler, called out for an attraction or a land right along its bend. New Orleans made a perfect fit adjacent to Frontierland, as in its heyday of a century ago it was, in Walt's words, "The Gay Paree of the American frontier."

The grandeur of the Crescent City plays out in this concept by Dorothea Redmond.

Hurry Up and Wait

In the tradition of the greatest Imagineering efforts, New Orleans Square went through several changes on its way from the drawing board to the Park. The concept started circulating at WED in the late 1950s, and soon incorporated many of the elements you find here now, but some were envisioned very differently at that point. Two walk-through attractions, a Haunted *House* and a Pirates *Wax Museum*, were being developed for the site. The overall framework of the land was soon in place in Disneyland. Included in this early frenzy of construction activity was the imposing facade of The Haunted Mansion show building. This structure cast a huge shadow over New Orleans Square for several years—from 1963 through the opening of the attraction in 1969—hinting at haunts to come with a sign posted on the attraction gates teasing Park Guests by inviting spirits to join in the fun. The site sat dormant while the Imagineers turned their focus toward the 1964-1965 New York World's Fair, and then as they developed and re-developed the show concept over a period of years after Walt's passing. The lessons learned from the Fair effort had a tremendous impact on the final attraction designs, particularly relating to people-moving.

An evocative pencil-sketch elevation by Herb Ryman

QUICK TAKE

• The mayor of New Orleans was on hand for the dedication of the land, and commented that it looked just like its namesake. He was somewhat miffed when Walt pointed out that the Disneyland version was cleaner.

Building facade elevations by Herb Ryman

A raucous pirate's den in this concept by Marc Davis

Johnny Come Lately

Pirates of the Caribbean in Disneyland was one of the last attractions overseen by Walt, though he did not live to see it open. Originally conceived as a walk-through wax museum in a much smaller space, Walt expanded it and converted it into a water ride after construction was already under way, so that boats could carry more Guests through a larger show space. From its opening in 1967, it has represented the epitome of the WDI themed show and has been added to our parks in Orlando, Tokyo, and Paris.

Even a classic can be enhanced, however. The runaway success of the 2003 film *Pirates of the Caribbean: The Curse of the Black Pearl*—inspired by the Disneyland original—created the likelihood that an entire generation of Park visitors would first learn of the world of these pirates through the film, not the attraction. These Guests would be disappointed not to encounter Captain Barbossa or Captain Jack Sparrow. So in 2006, these characters from the films were interwoven into the existing story, all the while ensuring that the spirit of the show remained intact.

Concepts for the 2006 enhancements by Chris Turner illustrate how the new show elements were integrated.

A Circuitous Route

Pirates of the Caribbean went through many iterations in the concept phase before becoming the attraction Guests know today. Walt initially had reservations about pirates as the subject matter of a Disney attraction, but found in Marc Davis the perfect artist to bring these rogues to life in a way that imbued them with charm and wit enough to make them appealing to Guests. The advent of Audio-Animatronics changed Walt's thinking on the original wax museum idea, and the experience gained at the 1964-1965 New York World's Fair regarding transportation of Guests led to the use of bateaux in the waterway.

This singing trio…er, quartet of pirates elicits a grin at first sight thanks to the skilled hand of Marc Davis.

QUICK TAKES

• The Auctioneer is voiced by Paul Frees—the Ghost Host in The Haunted Mansion and the narrator for Adventure Thru Inner Space.

• Pirates of the Caribbean in Disneyland features two waterfall drops rather than the one in Walt Disney World. While both are required to move Guests outside the parks' berms, the Florida version cannot go as deep because of the extremely high water table in the area.

• Johnny Depp contributed to his dialogue for the figures added to the show in order to ensure that his character was true to the films.

The mystery of the tropical islands is portrayed in this concept by Marc Davis.

The facade of The Haunted Mansion in a concept by Sam McKim and Ken Anderson

Scared Silly

Clearly one of the most popular attractions in the Park, both for the Imagineers and for our Guests, is The Haunted Mansion, which opened in 1969. Who can forget the first time you heard the immortal phrase, "Welcome, foolish mortals"? That first time is practically a *ride* of passage for every young Guest. Our Mansion is a mix of the frightening and the frightfully funny, a balance struck almost as much by accident as by plan. Without Walt to lead the creative effort, two competing points of view developed for the design. Marc Davis, who worked primarily on the characters and gags, wanted a lighter, more playful approach. Claude Coats, a former background painter who focused on settings and atmosphere, favored a darker tone. In the end, the characters are given life (or afterlife) by the contrast between the gags and the beautiful, darkly rendered environments.

The Haunted Mansion is the only Disney attraction to appear in a different land in each of the first four "Disneyland" Parks worldwide. This is a result of varying cultural factors, differing attraction mixes in the lands, and exciting ideas for a new spin on a classic. It's a testament to the original design, and to the ingenuity of the WDI design teams that found new and different ways to re-imagine the venerable Mansion.

The Haunted Mansion in Disneyland is set in an Antebellum manor for New Orleans Square while the Magic Kingdom Park version is based on nineteenth-century Hudson River Dutch Gothic architecture, owing to its Liberty Square setting. The Tokyo Disneyland Mansion looks like the one in Florida even though it's part of Fantasyland, while we opted for a rustic Western clapboard house for Phantom Manor in Frontierland in Disneyland Paris.

Concepts for new effects by Chris Turner

Our Favorite New Haunts

The Haunted Mansion has always been on everyone's list of must-see attractions, but that doesn't stop us from plussing the show. We love the classic—and sometimes amazingly simple—effects, but we always have new tricks up our sleeves. It has become our habit to rework the show when it comes back up from its annual "Nightmare Before Christmas" overlay—mounted each fall by our partners at Disney Creative Entertainment—with new and surprising additions. Recent "new magic" includes Madame Leota's head floating around the seance room in her crystal ball and a refined story line told through a thoroughly reworked attic scene.

QUICK TAKES

• The wonderful "Grim Grinning Ghosts" theme song was written by X Atencio, a former animator who got into songwriting only because Walt told him he'd be good at it. In addition to this song and the narration for The Haunted Mansion, X is also known for his work on "Yo Ho (A Pirate's Life for Me)" in Pirates of the Caribbean.

• A Guest with an affinity for word jumbles may spot tombstones in the graveyard scene bearing the names of Imagineers who worked on the attraction. *F. Regreoj* is art director Fred Joerger and *H. Snrub* is Harriet Burns, two of the three original members of the WED Model Shop.

• While voiced by Eleanor Audley, the role of Madame Leota was played by WDI's own Leota Toombs. Leota's daughter, Kim Irvine, also an Imagineer, plays the same role in the "Nightmare" overlay.

Haunting Lands . . . The Mansion frightens different neighborhoods worldwide

Disneyland Park	Magic Kingdom Park	Tokyo Disneyland	Disneyland Paris
New Orleans Square	**Liberty Square**	**Fantasyland**	**Frontierland**

I Hear Something Ringing in My Ears

As you wait for the train in New Orleans Square, you might think you hear a strange clicking sound emanating from the adjacent station. It's not your imagination. It's the tapping of a telegraph machine in the office, transmitting the first two lines of Walt Disney's dedication speech from the Opening Day of Disneyland. That station, incidentally, stood in for a Civil-War era train depot in a film segment for The American Adventure in Epcot in Walt Disney World.

Concept by Dorothea Redmond for a New Orleans Square interior

Artful Hand

Many of the illustrations that brought New Orleans Square to life were produced by Dorothea Redmond, a talented and versatile art director who came to WED from the world of filmmaking. Her graceful lines and eye for detail captured the very specific charm of the great city of New Orleans. She was instrumental in developing the Blue Bayou restaurant, the legendary Club 33 private dining spot, and the larger Disney family apartment over Pirates of the Caribbean that eventually became the Disney Gallery and now the Disneyland Dream Suite. She went on to exert a great deal of influence on World Showcase in Epcot.

Ships' masts peek over the rooftops of New Orleans Square

Ahoy, There!

Clearly, such a collection of pirates could only be found in a port city, right? And that's exactly what New Orleans is supposed to be. We have our river, but there was a desire to imply access to a much larger body of water nearby. How do we do that without having a large expanse of coastline and a view out over the Gulf of Mexico? By taking advantage of sightlines, and implying spaces and objects that we don't have the room to actually build. By placing a set of ship's masts with sails on the rooftops of the show building, we hint at an unseen dock. It is this sort of layering of scenes that gives depth and realism to the locales represented in the Park, and invites Guests to go exploring to discover the extent of it.

The balconies shown in these pictures demonstrate the work of WDI's prop designers and set decorators, who put so much thought into who "lives" in this place. We see the instruments of a musician, the afternoon tea set out for a socialite, and little hints of the Creole culture put out by a longtime resident.

65

Forced Perspective

A Different Perspective, Entirely

New Orleans Square provides the perfect backdrop for a discussion of forced perspective—a theatrical design technique whereby the designer plays with scale in the real world in order to affect the perception of scale in an illusory world. We all carry with us a sixth-sense understanding of relative scale, and it is that familiarity that allows Imagineers to trick us by changing the "rules." Buildings, props, or set pieces are built with size relationships that might be incorrect in order to increase the apparent size or distance of an object or space.

Cafe Orleans, with its clearly delineated balconies defining each floor, provides a very direct example of this practice. The ornate ironwork of the delicately detailed handrails and balustrades is carefully scaled down from the bottom floor to the top in order to squeeze three stories into a building that is less than three stories tall. In fact, the external indicators of each story such as windows and balconies do not always line up with the corresponding floors inside the buildings.

Forced perspective can be found around all the Disney parks. It is found in large exterior spaces and in smaller interior sets and models. It's just another way in which the world you encounter here in the Park might not be exactly as it appears. Some of the most often cited examples of forced perspective are found right here in Disneyland. Each building on Main Street, U.S.A., with few exceptions, is built with floors that diminish in height in order to make them appear taller than they really are without making the whole of Main Street too large and impersonal. One exception is Main Street Opera Hall, which was built full size in order to mitigate the potential visual intrusion from Tomorrowland off to the east. Also, the train station is necessarily full scale, as the upper floor is actually used by Guests. This also serves the function of obscuring the view from the main entrance into the Park toward the Castle—until we wish to reveal it.

Forced perspective does not follow any hard-and-fast rules. There isn't a formula that tells the designer to make one floor a certain percentage of the floor below. It's an art that is learned over time and whose implementation revolves around a number of different variables. The distance from which a building will be viewed, the proximity of other buildings, the functional height required inside, and the architectural references upon which a design is based will all be taken into account when determining the ideal scale for a building in a Disney park. Landscape design can also play a factor, and may be planted in a particular way so as not to spoil the illusion. We may also need to scale down our propping for these smaller spaces.

Third story 7 feet, 11 inches

Second story 8 feet, 9 inches

First story 13 feet

This diagram demonstrates the principle of forced perspective as applied to Cafe Orleans in New Orleans Square. Each floor is a bit smaller than the floor below, making a three-story building a bit more comfortable in scale.

Take a homespun tour through the nooks and crannies of the forests where all your favorite friends are found. You'll splash down into a briar patch and go chasing adventures with that silly ol' bear. Come to Critter Country to find your laughin' place.

Bears Are Critters, Too

Critter Country marquee concept by Guy Vasilovich

The current Critter Country has had perhaps more different addresses than any other real estate in the Park. Originally a portion of Frontierland, in the early days it was home to the Indian Village. Upon the installation of Country Bear Jamboree in 1972, this little patch was re-christened Bear Country, in keeping with its new character as a home to a band of singing bears, and somewhat distancing it from the more straightforward presentation of the Old West in the remaining sections of Frontierland. It became, in essence, a fantasy-based extension of the themes of the American frontier. When some new friends moved into the neighborhood with the 1989 addition of Splash Mountain, the new theme had to be broadened to make way for a wider array of animals—critters, even. This expansion of the story allowed for the later introduction in 2003 of the playful denizens of the Hundred Acre Wood, in The Many Adventures of Winnie the Pooh.

Town facade elevation by Dorothea Redmond

A Softer Face

When a land comes into being as an extension or reworking of an existing one, we need to make design changes to fit the new story line. Critter Country has evolved over time, differentiating itself from its original identity as a part of Frontierland. Originally this involved a softening of the style of the Frontierland facades, involving larger, more cartoony graphics and a brighter color palette. The landscape tends toward being a bit more indicative of northern climes, rather than the Southern or Southwestern motifs that dominate Frontierland. Over time, the addition of the landmark of Splash Mountain and the charm of the Hundred Acre Wood combined to change the face of Critter Country and give it a character all its own.

QUICK TAKES

• During the conversion to Bear Country and Critter Country, through the installation of Splash Mountain and all the other work in the area, the designers have maintained the Briar Patch store in its current location. It is an element that dates back to Walt's time, and was originally the Indian Trading Post.

• Critter Country extends a progression that makes its way around the Rivers of America from the entry to New Orleans Square east. These elements of the Park's Southern locales follow a path from the core of the city to the outlying plantations all the way out to bayou country.

• Fowler's Harbor was a recognition from Walt for Admiral Joe Fowler, a retired Navy officer who came on board to build Disneyland and later led the Disney efforts for the 1964–1965 New York World's Fair and the original construction of Walt Disney World.

Our Laughin' Place

Splash Mountain concept by Dan Goozee

Splash Mountain, added to the former Bear Country in 1989, is based on the 1946 Disney film *Song of the South*, which in turn was based on characters created by Joel Chandler Harris. With a mix of live action and animation, the movie related the stories of Brer Rabbit, Brer Fox, and Brer Bear as told by Uncle Remus. Our attraction, a singsong trip through pastoral Southern settings and a big splash down into the briar patch—or laughin' place, depending on your point of view— captures the charm and wonder of those stories. And Chickapin Hill adds another great silhouette to the skyline of the Park.

As is typically the case, the idea to do the attraction was a result of the alignment of several elements. This time it was the need to increase utilization of a little-used corner of the Park, the operators' long-standing interest in bringing a log-flume ride to Disneyland, and the impending closure of the America Sings attraction in Tomorrowland. The idea struck Imagineer Tony Baxter during a particularly eventful morning commute, and all the pieces fell into place, wrapped around the stories from *Song of the South*, which happened to feature lots of animal characters that were of a similar build to those in America Sings. All of the figures from that attraction made their way into Splash Mountain with the exception of a couple of geese that ended up in Star Tours.

True to its link to that musical review, Splash Mountain also offers a selection of great songs from the classic film it's based upon. Tunes like "How Do You Do?," "Everybody's Got a Laughing Place," and the Academy Award-winning "Zip-A-Dee-Doo-Dah" convey the story, brighten the mood, and put a bounce in your step long after you've left the attraction. The effect of a great song on an attraction and on the entire Disney park experience can never be overstated.

America's Still Singing

Splash Mountain finale concept by Collin Campbell

The outgoing America Sings gave Splash Mountain many of the Audio-Animatronics figures it needed in order to make the project feasible as well as a big finale scene that might otherwise never have been conceived. When the team did their inventory of scenes and characters and compared it to what they had available, there were extra figures. So the suggestion came to add a riverboat full of singing critters.

America Sings characters by Marc Davis that now make their home in Splash Mountain

QUICK TAKES

• The climactic drop into the Briar Patch is fifty-two feet down a forty-seven-degree incline.

• The "mountain" is eighty-seven feet tall, so as not to overwhelm the scale of the surrounding structures or of the Park itself.

• Splash Mountain has since been built in Magic Kingdom Park and in Tokyo Disneyland. At the latter location, it sparked the introduction of a whole new land—an extension of Westernland (their version of Frontierland), also called Critter Country.

The Many Adventures of Winnie the Pooh

Attraction entry concept by John Stone

Hunny, This Is One Sweet Ride

One of the most popular collections of stories in the entire Disney canon is the series of Winnie the Pooh films inspired by the writings of A.A. Milne. After bouncing around (conceptually) for years, this attraction finally landed in Critter Country in 2003. In theory, this attraction could have made its way into Fantasyland, or possibly even a neighborhood extension of Mickey's Toontown. But in the end, the folksy charm of the gang from the Hundred Acre Wood landed in this corner of the Park, where every critter is friendly and inviting. The addition of Pooh and all of his friends to this site, formerly occupied by Country Bear Jamboree, offered us the opportunity to broaden our cast of critters, further rounding out the core story line of this land. So we get to buzz along in our beehive to see what that silly ol' bear's been up to.

Scene concept by Steve Abernathy

Paint elevations for the Heffalumps and Woozles scene by Kirsten Ruhs. These images show the level of detail that must be communicated to field teams re-creating designs at full scale—sometimes halfway around the world.

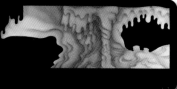

Critters Only, Please

Even the broad definition of Critter Country didn't allow Pooh and company to bring *all* of their friends along. Just the ones who were technically critters. Any references to Christopher Robin or the original setting of the stories in England were pared away, leaving only a woodsy playground. This way, these forest friends are still at home in our land, which must maintain its transitional relationship to Frontierland.

Paint elevation by Kirsten Ruhs

QUICK TAKE

• The previous attraction in this venue, Country Bear Jamboree, was an Audio-Animatronics show that ran in Disneyland from 1972 to 2001. An observant rider might spot the silhouettes of some former stars of that show over their shoulder as they enter the birthday scene—just hangin' around enjoying the view.

Color board for honeycomb ride vehicle by Lisa Galipeau

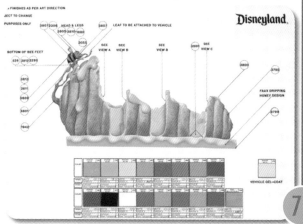

FANTASYLAND

Fantasyland is a gateway to the world of make-believe. Faraway kingdoms and adventures in imaginary realms lie around every corner. You can live out your daydreams and look into the windows of your childhood. It's a place where you can dream like a child no matter your age.

Setting the Scene

Bird's-eye view of Fantasyland by Bill Martin

One Man's Dreams

The most magical land of them all is Fantasyland—the heart and soul of Disneyland. Fantasy has always been a key element in the Disney pantheon. Fantasyland wraps all of the hopes and dreams of children around the world into the storybook settings they have read about in books and seen in the fairy tales re-told in the Disney animated films. It is a place of endless enchantment, where it's always "happily ever after" and the most direct translation of the most quintessentially Disney films. The moments that are re-created from those films appeal to the child in all of us like perhaps no other experiences in Disneyland and take us back to a time in our lives when make-believe was believable.

Fantasyland street facades

Mr. Toad's Wild Ride and Pinocchio's Daring Journey elevations by Ron Bowman

Take Two

Fantasyland has seen one major makeover—completed in 1983—during which much of the original medieval-tournament-tent look was replaced with a truer storybook expression, full of character, detail, and texture, just as Walt always said he had intended to build originally, but couldn't because of time and budget constraints. Led by Tony Baxter, a crew of young Imagineers worked with veterans Rolly Crump and Ken Anderson to realize the original vision. The attractions were updated, adding new exterior facades and entries. Each of the dark rides was lengthened by about twenty-five percent. Several exterior shows were relocated in the interest of improving circulation. King Arthur Carrousel was moved farther from the castle. Mad Tea Party was uprooted and placed closer to the Alice in Wonderland attraction. The Pirate Ship and Skull Rock Lagoon were removed to make way for a relocated and redressed Dumbo the Flying Elephant.

Straight from the Source

Ken Anderson was the first animator enlisted by Walt to work on precursors to Disneyland, beginning with his drawings for the Disneylandia miniatures. Ken had created a distinguished body of work as an animator and art director on many of the films portrayed throughout Fantasyland, but also had a background as a trained architect, so Walt had something else in mind for him. Ken was particularly well suited for the task of translating the fantastical environments of the films into the real world in a buildable form. His work at WED was pivotal in defining the Fantasyland style.

Sleeping Beauty Castle

Concept by Herb Ryman for Sleeping Beauty Castle

A Proper Centerpiece

Castles hold great iconic value for Disney. Our castles are some of our most powerful images—along with Mickey Mouse and perhaps Tinker Bell with her pixie dust. A castle was always at the heart of Walt's plans for Disneyland, and was used from the beginning in his attempts to explain the Park to his audience.

Sleeping Beauty Castle was first illustrated by Herb Ryman, who admitted that his design was heavily influenced by the styling of Mad King Ludwig's Neuschwanstein Castle in Bavaria because he happened to have reference material on that amazing structure handy when he was in a hurry to get the drawings ready for potential investors for Disneyland. He later tried to talk Walt into diversifying the design and pulling in additional references. Other elements made their way in, but Neuschwanstein clearly remains the primary inspiration.

Sleeping Beauty Castle also gives us some hints at Walt's particular brand of showmanship. It actually began life as Snow White's Castle—after Walt's original princess—which explains its rather Romanesque proportions and detailing. But *Sleeping Beauty* was in development at the animation studio during the time the Park was being built, and Walt saw the opportunity to use Disneyland to raise awareness of the upcoming film. The Sleeping Beauty diorama walk-through formerly located inside debuted in 1957, two years before the movie took its first bow.

Concept by Herb Ryman for Sleeping Beauty Castle courtyard

Castles in the Sky

Castle Courtyard concept by Herb Ryman

Herb Ryman, consummate WDI artist, is responsible for both Cinderella Castle in Magic Kingdom Park and for Sleeping Beauty Castle in Disneyland. It was Herb whom Walt called upon to produce some of the earliest concept artwork to capture the look of this particularly whimsical place. Herbie's architectural knowledge and innate sense of visual communication made it clear that these imaginary worlds could be built in such a way that would make them believable and evoke the essence of the storytelling that Walt wanted to achieve.

QUICK TAKES

• Sleeping Beauty Castle was originally designed—much in the manner of the Hollywood sets of the day—using standard architectural detail call-outs of pieces and parts available from studio shops around town.

• The top portion of the Castle originally faced the other way, toward the park entrance, until one day when Herb Ryman rearranged the model just prior to a review with Walt. Herb hadn't liked the way it had been designed, and thought the courtyard should face the rear. Walt walked into the WED model shop and immediately preferred the new way Herb had placed it.

Architectural elevation of Sleeping Beauty Castle

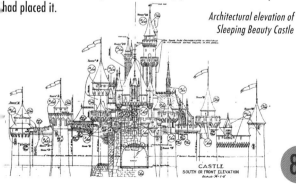

Early concept for King Arthur Carrousel by Bruce Bushman

Horsing Around

King Arthur Carrousel has one of the longest histories of any of our attractions. It is also one of the oldest Disney attractions anywhere in the world. King Arthur Carrousel was fabricated in 1922 by the Dentzel company and spent most of its early years in an amusement park in Canada before being discovered by Walt's designers during the construction of Disneyland and undergoing a thorough refurbishment. Some horses were re-designed so that they would all be running and augmented with more antique horses to make for a fourth row in addition to the original three. The carriages were removed and served as the basis for the train cars for the Casey, Jr., Circus Train.

Cinderella serves as the basis for the Magic Kingdom Park version. Disneyland Resort Paris has Le Carrousel de Lancelot, adhering more closely to the medieval legends for which the Park's European setting is famous. Tokyo Disneyland mimicked the Florida carrousel, but calls it Castle Carrousel and houses it under a different canopy. The carrousel in Hong Kong is very similar to the one in Disneyland, but is known as Cinderella Carousel.

Paint elevations by Bruce Bushman

New Dumbo atmosphere by David Negron

When I See an Elephant Fly

The magic of flight is prevalent in Fantasyland, and here it is geared toward our littlest "pilots." Dumbo the Flying Elephant is often the first attraction visited by a new young Guest and is consistently one of the most popular rides in the Park for tots, even though the film upon which it was based was first released way back in 1941. Dumbo the Flying Elephant was originally developed as a *take off* on the Pink Elephants sequence of the film. It was decided that this segment might be a bit too scary for small children, so that concept was re-thought.

The finials we added during the 1983 update were taken from a maquette for an abandoned Dumbo's Circus show concept. The team came across a Blaine Gibson maquette in storage, made a mold of the existing piece, and cast the finished finials for the Park at the same size.

Early Pink Elephants concept by Bruce Bushman

Maquette by Blaine Gibson for Dumbo's Circus

Early Peter Pan entry concept by Herb Ryman

Fly Boy

Who hasn't, at one time or another, dreamed of flying? The answer to that question goes a long way toward explaining the enduring appeal of Peter Pan's Flight. The story of the boy who can fly, from the 1904 play by J.M. Barrie that served as the inspiration for Walt's 1953 film, has captured children's imaginations for more than 100 years.

This attraction illustrates the type of thought that goes into the selection of each ride-vehicle system. With any attraction, the first step is to try to understand the story you want to tell and the particular *hook* that makes it interesting. For Peter Pan's Flight, we would want to fly through the show. So a system with an overhead track was devised—suspending the vehicle so that it can be carried through the show space as though flying under its own power. This choice dictates the sight lines available to Guests and, therefore, the staging of the show scenes. A designer typically doesn't have to worry about what a set looks like from the top, but in this case, it really matters.

Flying ship color elevation by Bruce Bushman

Peter Pan London mural concept by Tom Morris

Tally Ho!

Facade concept for Mr. Toad's Wild Ride by David Negron

Mr. Toad's Wild Ride is an example of a piece of source material—in this case, *The Wind in the Willows* segment from the 1949 animated film *The Adventures of Ichabod and Mr. Toad*—having value for us in the parks that outstrips its level of recognition with the typical Disneyland Guest. For us, if a film (in this case a short film) offers compelling characters and an attractive setting, it can become a story that can be told in a different medium. The world as seen through the eyes of one J. Thaddeus Toad is just plain fun. The Latin motto on the coat of arms says it all—*Toadi Acceleratio Semper Absurda*, or "Speeding with Toad is always absurd." After all, who hasn't insisted on sitting in the "driver's seat" while approaching the loading zone?

Mr. Toad entry mural by Ken Anderson

Mr. Toad story sketch

Snow White's Scary Adventures

Seven Dwarfs' Cottage concept by Ken Anderson

It's Dark in Here

Snow White's Scary Adventures is an example of one of our earliest forms for retelling the stories of our classic films, the Fantasyland dark ride. These wonderful attractions move Guests through the world of each film, presenting each story with a charming series of theatrical sets, moving flats, and ingeniously simple effects. The development of this genre was led by Ken Anderson, who created the ultraviolet painting technique we use in these shows. It's a mix of both black light and regular white light paint that can be shown under theatrical lighting as well as UV lighting to reveal different nuances of the art as the Guest moves through and the lighting changes. It requires that the artist producing the paint elevations work in a studio illuminated with ultraviolet light, to see the effects take shape. This technique is used to great effect in Snow White's Scary Adventures to heighten the sense of apprehension as our heroine makes her way through the forest. That tension was further enhanced during the 1983 remake, as the character of Snow White herself was added to the show for the first time; previously each guest *was* Snow White as they rode through the adventure.

This tower paint elevation by Kim Irvine shows one of the distinctive features of Snow White's Scary Adventures. The Evil Queen that is seen periodically through the window above the promenade gives Guests a hint of the story that awaits inside.

86

Pinocchio's Daring Journey facade by Jacques Charvet

Your Conscience "Nose" Best

The newest of the Fantasyland dark rides is Pinocchio's Daring Journey, which did not find a home in Disneyland until the revamp of Fantasyland in 1983. The ride through this classic film feels right at home, however, because the team followed all of the tried-and-true rules of the dark ride as they developed this relative newcomer.

Pinocchio's Daring Journey had the advantage of receiving the full exterior treatment from the outset, which allows us to start telling the story as soon as a Guest approaches. From the fanciful woodwork of the building facade—reminiscent of the craftsmanship on display

Jiminy Cricket maquette by Adolpho Procopio

in Geppetto's workshop—to the shapes and textures of the architectural detailing in the entry queue—which place us squarely in the Italian Alpine region where our story is set—every detail reinforces our placemaking. This approach makes Fantasyland a world of stories, brought to life through architecture, landscaping, and scenic design. There is a strong connection between the exterior appearance of a building and the experience that takes place inside.

Facade paint elevation by Kim Irvine

Casey, Jr., Circus Train

Concept by Bob Gurr for Casey, Jr.

The Little Engine That Could

While the current iteration of this attraction provides an element of thrill for younger riders (and not only for the opportunity to be labeled a "wild animal"), you'd be surprised to learn that Casey, Jr., Circus Train was originally designed to be Disneyland's first roller coaster. In the race for Opening Day, the original Imagineers planned to bring Casey, Jr., to life as a very thrilling experience woven through the hills surrounding Fantasyland. But testing revealed concerns that the ride wouldn't fully pay off as a thrill attraction, and that in trying to straddle the line between a fun, childrens' ride and a more thrilling coaster, they may have set themselves up for maintenance problems down the road. They shut down the attraction immediately after opening, reworked a couple of the lift hills and down ramps, and re-opened two weeks later. They then got to work on adding show elements to flesh out this tamer ride experience and eventually solved the riddle of exactly what a Disneyland roller coaster would be.

Casey, Jr., Station concept drawn by Bruce Bushman

Concept by Bruce Bushman for an earlier version of the trip through Monstro's mouth

Canal Fleet

Storybook Land Canal Boats represent perhaps the most direct offshoot of Walt's earlier plans for Disneylandia. His interest in the miniatures that led to that concept are put on full display here, where we ride gondolas through charming representations of locales culled from the greatest animated films the Walt Disney Studio has created. The boats themselves are very much in keeping with the original Mickey Mouse Park plans, which featured a canal boat among its offerings.

Those miniatures have had, in turn, a great deal of influence on other parts of the Park. During the 1983 renovation of Fantasyland, the team relied heavily on the example set by the Storybook Land miniatures as they developed the full-size versions of these tiny places. The original drawings, by animator and Imagineer Ken Anderson, were wonderful interpretations of storybook forms, but had a real architectural grounding due to his studies in pursuit of his degree in architecture. The Toad Hall facade for Mr. Toad's Wild Ride, in particular, owes a real debt to Ken's earlier work in Storybook Land.

Concept for Snow White's Grotto by John Hench

With Sincerest Grotto-tude

Disneyland gets much of its noted charm from the sweet little off-the-beaten-path nooks and niches filled with the details that make the place so visually rich. Snow White's Grotto was added to the Park in 1961, after Walt commissioned the pieces. When the exquisite marble statues arrived, it was discovered that they had been drafted in different scales, making Snow White the same size as the Dwarfs. Walt then assigned John Hench to create an appropriate setting that would show them to their best advantage. He placed Snow White high on a hill, above a waterfall in a "forest" setting—another example of forced perspective.

Another grotto was later added near Sleeping Beauty Castle, this time to commemorate *The Little Mermaid*. So, the films that launched the first and second Golden Ages of Disney Animation each have a home here. It is symbolic of the way films "graduate" to Fantasyland once they've established their status as classics.

The Brothers Grin

Nearly every Guest leaves Disneyland humming the melody to some song they have heard during their day there. One of the most frequent sources of those great Disney songs is a team of two brothers, Richard and Robert Sherman. They've written music for some of Disney's great films—such as *Mary Poppins* and *The Jungle Book*—in addition to memorable theme-park tracks including "It's A Small World (After All)" and "There's a Great, Big, Beautiful Tomorrow" from Carousel of Progress. On a drive with Walt from WED to the Studio lot, they were so caught up in the spirit of the message of "it's a small world" and their desire to do something for the beneficiary of the attraction, that they pledged to donate their earnings to UNICEF. Walt stopped the car and told them, "Boys, that song is going to put your kids through college!" And they say he was right!

Concepts by Bruce Bushman bring fantasy elements to life.

Merry Maker

Many aspects of the wonder and whimsy of the original Fantasyland were developed by the hand of Bruce Bushman. A superb draftsman, this versatile designer had a knack for translating fantastical film elements and story points into real-world experiences that captured the spirit of their inspirations entirely. He had a particular skill for finding the perfect moment from a film to build those experiences around. It is not always as simple a solution as it appears after the fact when one views the finished attraction. There are often several possibilities to sift through and assess before landing on the proper solution and developing the concept.

Aspiring to Greatness

This golden spire, which looks a bit out of step stylistically, relative to the rest of the architecture of the structure, actually has a grounding in historical fact. It was added to the design for the castle at Walt's request after he heard a story while he was on a tour of Notre Dame cathedral in Paris. It is a replica of a spire that was added to Notre Dame in the mid-1800s (roughly 500 years after the completion of the original construction) by the noted French architect Eugène Viollet-le-Duc, offered as an "improvement" to the original architecture.

91

Matterhorn Bobsleds

Walt looking over a model of Disneyland's first mountain

Climbing the Mountain

Imagineers are often asked how we make decisions as to what to add to our parks. Usually the answer is not a simple one. Matterhorn Bobsleds is a great example of how Disneyland can evolve—often very rapidly—based on a variety of factors. Challenges and opportunities present themselves all the time, and the key to the Imagineering mentality is to always look for ways to turn those things into positive changes for the Park. The Matterhorn story illustrates how that sort of thinking creates landmarks of Disneyland magic.

At its opening, the Park featured a twenty-foot-high mound of dirt formed by the digging of the Castle moat during Park construction. The pile had been dressed up with a bit of landscaping and some benches, and over the years had taken on the name Holiday Hill after an abandoned concept for the area. This hill was also the home to a rather unattractive steel tower for the Skyway buckets that made their way across the Park at that time. Additionally, Walt was still in search of a thrill attraction for Disneyland after the re-focusing of the Casey, Jr., Circus Train away from being a true roller coaster.

So, with all of this rattling around in the back of his mind, Walt found himself during a European vacation on the set of the 1959 film, *Third Man on the Mountain*, filmed atop the legendary Matterhorn in Switzerland. Around this time, an executive in Disneyland sent him a magazine article about wild-mouse-style roller coasters, and Walt's grand scheme was hatched. The skyline of the Park was forever changed, and our pattern for plussing the Park by identifying all of our best "opportunities" was set in place.

Not Yeti

The Abominable Snowman found within the Matterhorn offers a view into the evolution of our Audio-Animatronics figures—a lineage that leads eventually to the massive beast found inside Expedition: Everest in Disney's Animal Kingdom Park at Walt Disney World. The Abominable Snowman was added to Matterhorn Bobsleds in 1978 in keeping with WDI's desire to incorporate story elements into our thrill attractions, such as Big Thunder Mountain Railroad and Space Mountain. In Everest, the relative scale, menacing movements, and the ferocity of the modern figure show how far we have advanced the technology in the intervening years. However, the use of the element of surprise ensures that the original beast still packs a wallop!

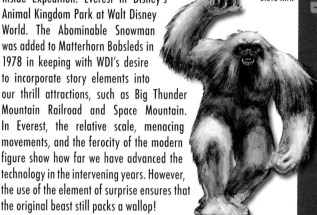

Concept sketch by Steve Kirk

QUICK TAKES

• Matterhorn Bobsleds was the first tube steel-track roller coaster in the world when it premiered in 1959.

• Matterhorn Bobsleds was originally part of Tomorrowland, but made its way into Fantasyland in the early 1970s without moving an inch.

• The Disneyland Matterhorn is 147 feet tall, exactly $\frac{1}{100}$ the size of the actual mountain.

Matterhorn Mountain looms over Fantasyland in this concept by Herb Ryman

Wonderland peeks outside the show building in this sketch by Tony Baxter

Alice Through the Wall of the Show Building

In 1951 the Walt Disney Studios turned the story of *Alice in Wonderland* into a full-length animated feature. Walt had been interested in the original source material for some time, dating back to his early "Alice" comedies—a series of shorts based on the Lewis Carroll book that featured a live-action Alice placed into an animated Wonderland. He produced these films in the latter days of one of his earlier ventures—Laugh-O-gram Films in Kansas City—prior to his move to Hollywood, and always maintained an affinity for them.

Late, Late, for a Very Important Date!

Much like the full-length feature version of *Alice in Wonderland*, which was in development at the Studio for the better part of two decades, this attraction went through some growing pains. The original version of the show was planned to be an Opening Day attraction in Disneyland, but due to time and budget constraints, it had to be tabled for later. Three years later, to be exact.

Inside Out

During the rebuilding of the attraction in 1983, the loop of exterior track was added. It's a wonderful kinetic element that connects it to the relocated Mad Tea Party and allows Guests outside a glimpse at the ride. Plus, it's quite a thrill for big and little kids alike to swing the nose of that caterpillar out over the edge of those great big leaves.

Queen of Hearts maquette by Peter Kermode

Aerial view of Mad Tea Party by Bruce Bushman

A New Spin on an Old Story

Mad Tea Party offers an even more whimsical take on *Alice in Wonderland*. One of the most memorable moments in the story was the zany tea-party scene, attended by Alice and her frantic new acquaintances. Imagineers looked for a suitable basis for a pleasant little outdoor diversion, and found it in this scene. Guests approach the tea party much the way Alice did. The March Hare's quaint little house is off to the side, housing the attraction's control booth. Japanese tea lanterns add to the festive air of the occasion. The experience captures the madcap—or rather, mad*cup*—nature of Alice's adventures in Wonderland, and one imagines she felt something of the same sense of disorientation by the end of the tea party that we may feel at the end of a few good spins around the turntable.

The relocation of Mad Tea Party in a concept by David Negron

"it's a small world"

The exuberance of "it's a small world" is captured in this scene concept by Marc Davis.

it's a big idea, after all

Few attractions embody the meaning of "theme" park better than "it's a small world." This enchanting voyage around the globe captures a simple, but profound idea—that the children of the world understand our commonalities and can create a harmonious future—captures its essence perfectly with a sweet and sincere (and catchy) song, and offers an artwork style that tells that story as beautifully as words ever could. The song was written by Richard and Robert Sherman after the original plan to feature all of the various national anthems proved unwieldy.

"it's a small world" debuted at the 1964-1965 New York World's Fair, as the centerpiece of a pavilion to honor the United Nations Children's Fund (UNICEF). The attraction was completed in less than a year, after Walt reversed course upon learning that someone within the company had initially turned down the request by saying that WED was too busy with efforts already under way for the Fair. Upon completing its run in New York, the original attraction was relocated to Disneyland, and has since been replicated at each of the Magic Kingdom parks worldwide.

Concept elevations for "it's a small world" by Mary Blair

Concept for the relocation of "it's a small world" to Disneyland by Johno Lim

QUICK TAKES

• The Disneyland installation of "it's a small world" opened in 1966, and currently features 297 dolls and 256 toys representing six continents and singing the famous song in five languages.

• The trees planted on the roof mask the mass of the show building, maintaining the intimate scale of Fantasyland. This was a happy accidental discovery in the WED Model Shop when some trees were left on top of the model prior to a review with Walt.

Mary Blair Flair

Scene concept by Mary Blair

"it's a small world" is one of the purest evocations in three dimensions of the distinctive style of Mary Blair—animation color stylist, Imagineer, Disney Legend, and reportedly Walt's favorite artist. Mary's wonderful color studies and background layouts with their childlike innocence made her a perfect fit for the assignment of designing "it's a small world." You may see stylistic links to some of her other prominent work in the films *Cinderella*, *Alice in Wonderland*, *Peter Pan*, and *The Three Caballeros*.

97

MICKEY'S TOONTOWN

Mickey's Toontown is your chance to meet the characters where they live. You'll be "drawn" into an animated world and become a Toon for a day. Be sure to visit Mickey's house and take a spin with Roger Rabbit. Just don't forget to "Squash" and "Stretch" on your way in!

Bird's-eye concept of Mickey's Toontown by Nina Rae Vaughn

This Land Can Carry a Toon

Disneyland is filled with opportunities to visit the settings of our favorite stories. But before 1993, our favorite classic cartoon characters never actually had their own prime real estate. Mickey's Toontown came along to remedy that, and take our Guests into the world of animation, particularly of the animated short. Haven't you always envisioned a place where those characters live and work, all existing together in a sort of madcap harmony?

This land captures the zany, anything-goes spirit that Disney animators have brought to their films for eight decades, with faces hidden in many of the building facades and gags strewn about everywhere. Everything here has a history to it, although that history plays itself out in humorous and inventive ways. From broken walls to fallen objects, and from talking doorways to upside-down right-side-up crates, everything here is active and establishes the notion of who lives here and how different a place it is. The architecture is squashed and stretched just like the animation technique applied to a character in motion. Sometimes the fun is in seeing how elements that are familiar to us from our "normal" world look from the point of view of a toon.

This land expanded the boundaries of Disneyland, pushing the Park farther to the north. It was necessary to tunnel under the existing railroad track to do this, and the rolling hills mask the very nearby elements of the outside world just beyond the Toontown perimeter.

Tooning In

Of the many storytelling devices that form the sources and inspirations for the "lands" in Disneyland, the central idea for Mickey's Toontown derived from the short cartoons that defined the Studio in its early days. In Disney terms, this style of animation is another of our core storytelling devices. It features a carefully crafted and unique sense of timing and visual design. Though this does not necessarily

Concept for Toontown Fire Station by Marcelo Vignali

embody a true theme in the same sense that the other lands do, it still fits within Disneyland because the films of this era all have a similar sensibility when it comes to the archetypal character design, their distinctive style of humor, the settings in which they tend to take place, and the nature of the stories told.

The gateway shown in an elevation by Don Carson tells us how to get to Toontown.

The distinctive skyline of Mickey's Toontown, as depicted in Don Carson's concept elevations.

Roger Rabbit's Car Toon Spin concept by Marcelo Vignali

Hailing a Cab

The 1988 film *Who Framed Roger Rabbit* was a shining example of the renaissance of Disney in the mid-to-late 1980s. The leadership of the company was spurring all the creative areas of the company to more and more ambitious efforts. *Who Framed Roger Rabbit* hearkened back to some of the great groundbreaking work done under the leadership of Walt Disney himself. It was a collaborative effort with Steven Spielberg's Amblin Entertainment, a mix of live action and animation using cartoon references that spanned the early days of the art form—both from Disney and from other studios. It captured the essence of those crazy characters and the situations in which they just can't seem to avoid finding themselves, and makes for a fun and zany attraction.

Short and Sweet

The act of designing a "dark ride" such as Roger Rabbit's Car Toon Spin is very similar to that of developing an animated short film. Many of the same techniques are brought to bear, and we go through many of the same steps in the process. We outline our story. We storyboard it. We spend time coming up with gags to make it fun. We integrate the visuals of the design with any dialogue needed to advance the action. We fine-tune (fine-*toon*?) our timing and pacing, and assess the payoff of the story. Even today, the Imagineers rely on the model set out for us by the animators of the Walt Disney Studios, especially those who made the transition from animation to Imagineering and created this whole new art form.

Roger Rabbit's Car Toon Spin concept by Marcelo Vignali

The essence of the film shows in story concepts for attraction scenes by Marcelo Vignali

Imagineers often play as they work, as demonstrated in this playful storyboard/concept drawing by Marcelo Vignali. The two jacks-in-the-box are caricatures of Marcelo and Joe Lanzisero ("M" and "J"), the executive and lead designers on Toontown and Roger Rabbit's Car Toon Spin.

Mickey and Minnie's Houses

Concept sketch for Minnie's house by Joe Lanzisero

Homes Sweet Homes

The most prominent citizens of Toontown, to be sure, are Mickey Mouse and his sweetheart, Minnie. When it comes to designing their homes, located on prime real estate near the heart of town, you have to keep the residents in mind. Each and every element of their houses is designed after their tastes and characteristics. The colors, shapes, and attitudes of each character are used as the stylistic guide for every piece of furniture, each prop, all the decorations on the wall, and the overall architectural treatment of the interiors as well as the exteriors.

Mickey and Minnie like to surround themselves with things that make them feel at home. Notice the cooking utensils, the sporting goods, the games, the lamps, and the clothes. Everything is designed to be a part of their world. These pieces sometimes blur the lines between prop design and show set production, but in the end we always figure out what's what.

Mickey's den concept by Don Carson

Concept sketch for Donald's Boat by Robert Coltrin

The Boat's Sprung a Leak!

Imagineers love to play with water, and especially love to find creative ways to get water on our Guests. It can be sprayed, splashed, squirted, dumped, dripped, and dropped, or any combination thereof. Here in sunny California, that often comes as a refreshing relief during the course of a long, hot day in the Park. Donald's Boat, the *Miss Daisy*, is a great excuse to get everybody wet, and the chaotic nature of the leaky boat plays well into Donald's frenetic personality.

Look closely and you can see that the boat itself is made up of design elements taken directly from Donald himself. The blue of his uniform and the yellow of his bill are both very prominently featured. The roof of the bridge even looks like Donald's cap, topping the whole thing off. The entire boat and the experience surrounding it are dimensional representations of the character of our character!

Donald's Boat color elevation by Joe Lanzisero

*Design intent elevations for Donald's
mailbox by Will Eyerman*

Concept = Reality

Sometimes, our concepts undergo a great deal of revision as they make their way from the drawing board to the Park. It's part of how we continue to plus things all the way through the production pipeline. Once we get to detail drawings—or design intent—however, we've got a very clear idea of what we're going for in the finished piece. In that case, the challenge is to guide each piece through the production pipeline while maintaining the vision that was captured in the design. It takes careful coordination by the fabrication team and relies on thorough and consistent communication from the designer and the art director. It's easy for unintentional changes to creep in over the course of that effort, so care is taken to ensure that doesn't happen.

Sky Lines

Designing Disney parks requires looking at every element from multiple viewpoints. When we finalize our layouts for areas of each park, we take into account many variables in order to ensure the harmonious and visually appealing environments that are our goal. We carefully place our elements so that the masses and focal points create a pleasing variety in the composition.

106

Yes, We Do Windows!

It makes sense that Toontown would have commemorative windows, just like Main Street, U.S.A. Here you'll find references to some of the heavy hitters in the world of animated shorts. We have the Chinny Chin Chin Construction Co., Three Little Pigs, Proprietors. There is the Huffin & Puffin Wrecking Co. headed up by the Big Bad Wolf—Retired. Of course, the whole thing is headed up by Laugh-O-gram Films, Inc., with a certain young Mr. W. E. Disney serving as the Directing Animator.

Gag Fest

Toontown lends itself to lots of built-in sight gags. They are encountered constantly as you walk around the land, just as they come when you're watching a short. For the designers, the fun lies in putting themselves into the mind of a Toon and trying to see the world through their eyes. We can draw from the classic gags that have been played out in the shorts, or come up with our own in the same vernacular. Either way, it gives us just the excuse we need to watch lots of cartoons. Hey, it's for work!

Dumbbell gag sketch by Don Carson

TOMORROWLAND

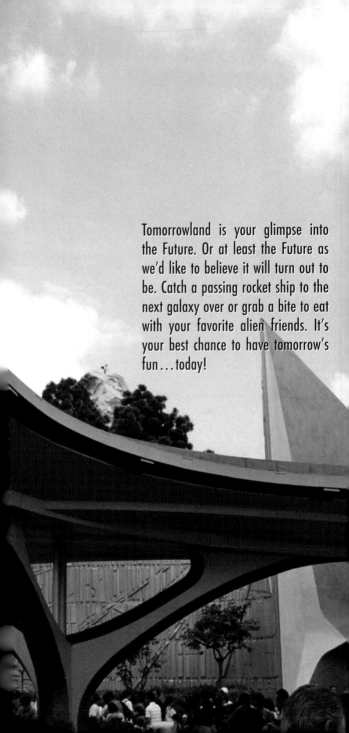

Tomorrowland is your glimpse into the Future. Or at least the Future as we'd like to believe it will turn out to be. Catch a passing rocket ship to the next galaxy over or grab a bite to eat with your favorite alien friends. It's your best chance to have tomorrow's fun...today!

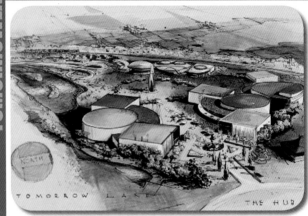

Tomorrowland overview by Herb Ryman

Tomorrow Is Another Day

Nothing changes faster than tomorrow. Before you know it, tomorrow is today, and our dreams of tomorrow have changed. Walt knew this, and faced it as an exciting challenge. No land in Disneyland has undergone as many changes (and extreme makeovers) as Tomorrowland. It's the fundamental challenge when you build something and call it *Tomorrow*land. There are many different visions of the future that we see in film, on television, in art, and in print. But it's just the sort of task Imagineers love to tackle.

Despite the heroic efforts of the early Imagineers and the entire Disneyland team, Tomorrowland was barely there on Opening Day. It was intended to be a new and exciting vision of the future (set in the then-incomprehensible *1986*), full of optimism and confidence in the abilities that Walt saw in the modern industry of his day. At its opening, Tomorrowland's design was driven largely by time constraints and funding. So, Tomorrowland did not truly receive the Imagineers' full focus until after the Park had opened, but they made up for lost time.

This mural by Scot Drake for the facade of Buzz Lightyear Astro Blasters captures the essence of Tomorrowland as an intergalactic gathering spot.

Tomorrowland featuring Space Mountain by Herb Ryman and John Hench

Change Is the Only Constant

As soon as he had a bit more money to work with (from the first few years of operating the Park), Walt began building ever-grander visions of the future. The first update of Tomorrowland in Disneyland took place in 1959, and subsequent updates in 1967 and throughout the mid-1980s continued the effort of staying ahead of the audience's growing expectations. The 1998 New Tomorrowland bucked this trend, after upper management challenged the Imagineers with an assertion that in the future, people would reject impersonal technology. So they envisioned a future with an earthy patina and a more naturalistic feel.

The current iteration owes its styling to the products of modern industrial design. In reviewing design touchstones from the past fifty years, the team realized that the items that held their own against changing tastes and styles tended to share common traits. The forms are kept clean with little superfluous ornamentation, but the finishes are varied through the application of a particular color and material palette. Often, the predominant color was white—timeless, optimistic, and not subject to the whims of color trends—with accents in blues and silvers, typically metallic. This motif was then applied throughout the land, which included returning Space Mountain to its classic white facade.

Star Tours

Concept by Gil Keppler for the Star Tours queue

Outside Influences

Upon its debut in Tomorrowland in 1987, Star Tours represented a radical departure for Disneyland, in more ways than one. It was the first attraction in the Park based on a story and imagery that had not originated with or been adapted by the Company. The Star Wars universe created by George Lucas and developed over the course of his immensely popular film trilogies was a cultural phenomenon that caught the attention of a group of young Imagineers who argued that Star Wars held the same place in the public's consciousness as the Disney films. They recognized that, at their core, the Star Wars stories were built upon the same elemental mythologies that formed the foundations of the best of Disney storytelling.

The Imagineers had been looking for some time for a way to make use of flight-simulator technology—moving platforms that use changing G-forces to mimic the motions of vessels in flight—but they had yet to find the proper concept. When the idea of a flight simulator was combined with the world of Star Wars, the Imagineers saw the perfect opportunity. After the proper simulator was located, the effort turned toward merging the needs of the story with all the elements that could be brought into the cabin to tell it. The window on the face of the ship provides the primary view to where we're going. At the suggestion of George Lucas, the rookie Audio-Animatronics pilot, Rex, serves as our comic relief. He drives the action, at times narrating as well. The "exterior" video feed shown on the monitors allows us to see R2-D2 monitoring the ship and to witness the destruction of the Death Star. All of these are timed and coordinated to provide a virtual 360-degree view of what's going on all around us.

Mural design by Gil Keppler for the Star Tours exterior

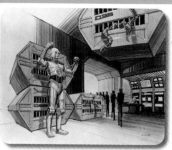

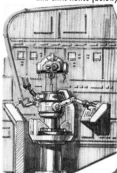

Existing and new characters were used in the show, as seen in these concept sketches by Gil Keppler (left) and Chris Runco (below).

Designers of Good Character

For Imagineers, the greatest tools to work with are a set of interesting and endearing characters and a fantastic environment in which to allow their stories to play out. The Star Wars universe offered both of these in abundance. For many Imagineers, the opportunity to work on a Star Wars project was a dream assignment within their dream job!

QUICK TAKES

- Star Tours has been replicated in Disney's Hollywood Studios (Florida), in Tokyo Disneyland, and in Disneyland Paris.

- The reference in the pre-show audio to "THX 1138" refers to the 1971 George Lucas science fiction film of the same name. It was his first feature-length film and is often referenced in his films, as well as those of other filmmakers. You'll also hear a certain "Egroeg Sacul" being paged from time to time (*hint* . . . try reading it backward).

- The two repair droids seen in the queue are made from the armatures of two Audio-Animatronics figures formerly in the cast of America Sings. Their voices were provided by WDI show writers Tom Fitzgerald and Mike West.

This illustration by Collin Campbell shows the audience view as the action plays out.

Space Mountain

Early Space Mountain concept by John Hench

It's a Blastoff

Space Mountain is one of the truly classic Disney attractions. One of the first E-Ticket attractions to make its debut in Walt Disney World rather than in Disneyland—in December 1974—it was a fairly radical idea when mentioned by Walt to John Hench in 1964. No one had tried placing a roller coaster inside a darkened building before, but it was a necessary part of the story. We needed to have the control over the lighting offered by being inside in order to convince a rider that he or she is hurtling through outer space, and we didn't want a typical, exposed roller coaster track to distract from the other stories we were telling in the surrounding area of Tomorrowland.

Space Mountain captures the spirit of the era in which it was originally designed, when the exuberance of the race for space had taken hold around the world (literally and figuratively). It was a time of great imagination regarding what awaited us out there. Space Mountain offers up a playful vision of a time when a journey off the planet might be as routine as your daily commute of today.

Space Mountain section/elevation

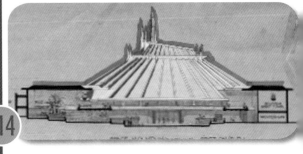

Beaming on the Outside

A key contribution to the distinctive look of Space Mountain came from John Hench when he saw the first schematic drawings that called for concrete beams to hold up the roof structure. Typical construction techniques would call for those beams to be placed on the inside of the building, with the roof surface applied on the outside. John insisted that the beams be put on the outside, for two reasons: it allowed for a smooth surface inside onto which a star field and meteors could be projected, and it created some forced perspective on the exterior as the columns converged toward the top of the building, increasing the apparent height of the structure. This look, designed over thirty years ago, still works as an image of the future, as it falls well outside the norm of what we tend to see during our day-to-day lives.

Space Mountain logo graphic by Fulton von Hagen

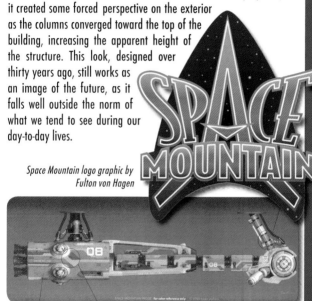

Color concept elevation by Owen Yoshino

QUICK TAKES

• During the 2004–2005 renovation of Space Mountain, the entire track was rebuilt, including digging up its foundation and replacing it with a new one stretching to a depth of fifteen feet below grade level.

• The musical accompaniment was written by Michael Giacchino, the same composer who wrote the score for *The Incredibles*.

Space Mountain Range . . . Blasting off around the world

Magic Kingdom Park	Disneyland Park	Tokyo Disneyland	Disneyland Paris	Hong Kong Disneyland
1974	1977	1983	1995	2005

Autopia

Concept by Eric Heschong for the 2000 renovation of Autopia

License to Thrill

What child doesn't want to drive a car? How will we teach the next crop of drivers the thrill of the open road? Those questions reveal the basis of the Autopia in all of its iterations over the years. This Tomorrowland staple has been offering a first driving experience to generations of young Guests.

When Disneyland opened, the interstate highway system was just being implemented. In keeping with his long-standing interest in education, Walt felt that Autopia could go a long way toward teaching kids how to drive on the new roadways. The original Autopia featured no guide rails, so the cars were constantly bumping into each other as they made their way around. Guide rails were, of course, quickly added to keep everybody on track. Unfortunately similar rails have still not made it to the Los Angeles freeways.

Concept sketch by Jason Hulst

Autopia was updated in 2000 to integrate it into New Tomorrowland. The designs of the new cars are intended to capture the character of three different types of cars and their drivers—one rugged, one sleek, one casual.

Car elevations by Jason Hulst

Concept design for Orbitron by Andrew Probert, later used for Astro Orbitor

Take It for a Spin

Serving as a kinetic beacon into the world of Tomorrowland is the Astro Orbitor. This attraction, a plussing of the original Astro Jets (later Rocket Jets), took on its current location and appearance in the New Tomorrowland redesign of 1998. With a new look inspired by the Orbitron in Discoveryland in Disneyland Paris, it now spins in the Central Plaza rather than its original spot atop the PeopleMover load platform. It serves as a beacon to the future and gives Tomorrowland the same visibility from the hub as Adventureland, Frontierland, and Fantasyland.

Astro Orbitor is a playful, exhilarating jaunt around the solar system, now with a styling motif that owes more to star charts and orbital patterns than the space-age industrial design that had been its previous basis. The spinning and twisting forms add to the thrill of the experience for those on board, and to the kinetics for those merely viewing this marvelous sculpture.

Astro Orbitor vehicle elevation by Andrew Probert

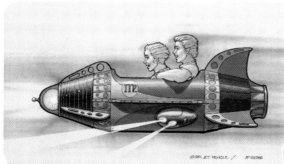

The Disneyland Monorail passes over the submarine lagoon in a concept by John Hench.

The Best Laid Plans of Mice and Imagineers

One source of the famous charm of Disneyland is its density and the wonderful complexity of its spaces. As it was the very first Disney park, the original designers of Disneyland had no prior experience upon which to draw. For example, they could not possibly have known just how successful the Park would turn out to be. They couldn't have guessed how many people would have to be accommodated by the pathways and attractions and transportation systems. As thrilled as they might have been by Walt's vision for the Park, nobody could know that it would thrive and continue to grow for decades on end, stretching the Park's footprint and extending its boundaries to add new capacity and experiences. Considering the novelty of the idea and the lack of relevant precedents, it is a marvel that the original master plan laid out by Walt and Marvin Davis and the rest of the early Imagineers was forward-thinking enough to allow for this growth.

The inventiveness borne of necessity has given the Park an intimacy and a series of spatial relationships that add to the experiences there. It plays out in Tomorrowland in ways both obvious and subtle—the confluence of vehicles in motion that have defined Tomorrowland for decades and the three-level terrace view with the suspended walkway at the exit of Space Mountain. As these elements were layered over time, the care with which they were placed and interwoven with the rest of the Park kept it from becoming a jumble of competing elements.

We see additional instances of this carefully controlled evolution in other lands. The effort to coordinate the entrances to Jungle Cruise and the Indiana Jones™ Adventure adds to the rich layering of Adventureland. And a flyover walkway moves Guests over the entrance to Pirates of the Caribbean and into New Orleans Square, creating a cozy courtyard and an appealing view from above.

Future Focused

Concept for Tomorrowland by John Hench

Tomorrowland, even after all these iterations, owes a great debt to John Hench, who was instrumental in establishing the particular brand of Disney futurism—in Tomorrowland, at the 1964-1965 New York World's Fair, and at Epcot. He was a close confidante of Walt's, and is perhaps second only to him in his influence on the art form that is the Disney park. Over the years, John contributed design and direction for parks around the world, and was an eloquent educator of generations of Imagineers regarding what the Disney parks are and what *exactly* makes them tick.

A Blast from the Past

Rising atop the building facades of Tomorrowland since 1998 is an object with a significant attachment to Disneyland history. It is a replica of the original Moonliner that made its home in the Park from 1955 through 1967—at one point a beacon for the Rocket to the Moon attraction—and always a bright, gleaming image of the optimistic future. And John Hench's design looks just as good today. The seventy-six-foot-tall original Moonliner was the tallest element in the Park at the time. The new version, part of our "Future That Never Was," is only sixty feet tall, but sits on an elevated platform to maintain its visual impact.

119

Finding Nemo Submarine Voyage

Concept by Chris Turner for the updated subs and lagoon

A Resurfacing Attraction

One of the major additions of the 1959 Tomorrowland overhaul was the Submarine Voyage. Walt loved the idea of being able to take his Guests to places (or times) they could never get to on their own, often via conveyances that were no longer in use or not accessible to the average person. Perhaps his second-most-prized collection (after his trains) was his fleet of submarines (which he once labeled the eighth-largest sub fleet in the world). He used these as vehicles to probe the depths of our imagination in the original show, a simulated trip to the North Pole beneath the polar ice cap, that ran until 1998.

The fleet was held in port for eight years between the time the original show was retired and the current show was introduced. As usual, the Imagineers wanted to wait until they had just the right story to tell, and they found it with Disney•Pixar's *Finding Nemo*, released in 2003. This film offered the perfect blend of wonderful characters and an underwater setting that was strong enough to raise the subs again. So Guests get to find Nemo all over again and revisit many of the key moments from the film.

The angler fish is chomping at the bit in this concept sketch by Chris Turner.

Finding Nemo Submarine Voyage

Concept for "Big Blue World" finale by Chris Turner

The Media Is the Message

Finding Nemo Submarine Voyage is a perfect example of the use of projected media to extend the world of an attraction beyond the built environment. In this instance, the design team took advantage of the carefully controlled vistas afforded by the portholes and the diffusion of the water that visually ties the real and projected scenery together. The computer-generated animation, provided by our partners at Pixar Animation Studios, creates expanded spaces and for the first time allows our characters to look, move, and act as they do in the feature film, which would be impossible for us to achieve using our current Audio-Animatronics mechanical technology.

QUICK TAKES

• In order to create the brilliant colors of the coral reef, Imagineer Susan Dain developed a technique of using crushed colored glass embedded in the paint in order to avoid the severe fading that would otherwise be inevitable in the harsh environment of heavily chlorinated water.

• Nowhere is the issue of show timing more critical than in the Finding Nemo Submarine Voyage. Not only is each Guest observing the show through a fairly small porthole in the wall of the sub, but we also have to account for the fact that we have twenty Guests sitting along each side of the sub. The audio tracks for the show are broken into four different show zones so that the Guests hear the portion of the show that relates to what they're seeing.

Storyboard sketches by Chris Turner

Concept by Chuck Ballew for Buzz Lightyear Astro Blasters

Round and Round and Round

Buzz Lightyear Astro Blasters opened in 2005 in the space formerly occupied by Circle-Vision 360 and takes us into the story-within-a-story from the two Toy Story films—the Gamma Quadrant as patrolled by the "real" Buzz Lightyear. We join forces with Buzz as he battles evil Emperor Zurg in his efforts to steal the batteries used to power toys. Once the story is set, it often leads us toward the proper format to tell the story. In the case of Buzz Lightyear Astro Blasters, our inspiration came from the world of modern video games, which led to one of our most interactive attractions. Of course, we wanted to make that genre function in a way that turns it into a group activity for the whole family to enjoy together. This whimsical, colorful, shooting-gallery-on-a-track allows Guests to influence the show. People feel more engaged with the story when it works both ways.

In developing this attraction, Imagineers made use of the traditional continuous-motion OmniMover system—like the one you'll find in The Haunted Mansion—with a new twist. This vehicle can spin a full 360 degrees entirely at the control of the Guest, while remaining in forward motion through the show scenes all the time. The engineering effort required to package that capability into a pre-existing ride system is a remarkable feat. The show-control system communicates with each vehicle continuously, and keeps track of each blaster's hits and scores in order to give players their "rank" upon exiting the attraction.

Magic Kingdom	Tokyo Disneyland	Disneyland Park	Hong Kong Disneyland	Disneyland Paris
1998	2004	2005	2005	2006

The in-your-face action of Honey, I Shrunk the Audience

In Order to Think Small You've Got to Think Big

How do you make a film more involving? By involving the audience in the film! When the action on-screen makes its way out into the theater, the viewer becomes engaged, reacting in a way that film alone cannot elicit. *Honey, I Shrunk the Audience* is an important step in our development of this kind of immersive experience. It was the first attraction to make use of large-scale mechanical effects—used to achieve the shaking of the room and the rumbling of the floor as we shrink to our supposed size—as well as effects built into the seat frames such as dog sneezes and mouse tails.

Making Places

Honey, I Shrunk the Audience is also a good place to talk about place-making. This is a prime function of WDI's designs, and a big reason that our shows are so successful. Place-making involves crafting a setting of time and place that will provide the appropriate backdrop to our shows. For this show, an entity—the Imagination Institute—was created as the host of the Inventor of the Year awards. This provides the backstory that brings us into the theater and the characters (and the relationships between characters) that will move the story forward. Had we simply dropped in the characters from the *Honey, I Shrunk the Kids* films, the show would have had no context to connect it to the rest of the Park.

3-D Times Three . . . All the past and present shows in this theater

Magic Journeys 1986	*Captain Eo* 1986–1997	*Honey, I Shrunk the Audience* 1998–????

Disneyland Monorail

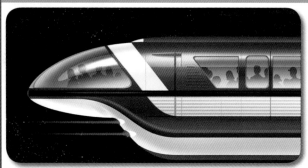

Monorail color elevation by Scot Drake

Positively Beaming

Perhaps the most striking and durable symbol of Tomorrowland's vision of the future is the Disneyland Monorail. From its inception, it has been a cornerstone element of this "Land on the Move." The streamlined form of its shell, the visually uncluttered look of the beam upon which it rides, and its quiet operation all conspire to inspire dreams of a better future through human ingenuity.

The Disneyland Monorail serves to convey the idea that we will always be looking forward and striving for new means of travel. That aspect of the monorail is key to understanding what Walt had in mind for Disneyland way back in 1959—that new transportation systems would provide the underpinnings of an entirely new type of city—essentially the idea that the carefully designed "city" of modern-day Walt Disney World represents.

In 2008, the fifth iteration of the Disneyland Monorail (the Mark VII) appeared in Tomorrowland, replacing the previous fleet. These new trains—spiritual successors to the Mark I—feature color-shifting paint schemes, tinted windows for comfort, and an outward-facing seating arrangement in order to offer unfettered views of all the sights there are to see along this very special route.

The Mark VII Monorail as rendered by Scot Drake

Innoventions is a key part of this concept for New Tomorrowland by Eric Heschong

Spinning Tales of the Future

Innoventions is the part of the Park in which we bring the future closer to the modern day. While it is thrilling and exciting to see visions of a future that might be decades or more away, the overall experience of a day in Tomorrowland would be a bit hollow if all it entailed were these far-off possibilities. Innoventions makes the future tangible, tactile, and fun. It's an opportunity to see how technological advances in various industries might affect the way we live our lives, do our jobs, and spend our playtime—in the near term.

It is inspired by the energy of a modern consumer-electronics expo, where we find something new and fresh around every corner. Exhibits are presented by some of the leading companies and trade organizations in modern industry. Our exhibits are designed to be active, enjoyable, informative, and clearly associated with our everyday lives. In this way, Innoventions takes on an overall story that is connected to—but also distinct from—the discrete story lines necessary to sustain each exhibit.

Innoventions fulfills Walt's vision of using his parks as a conduit for participating companies from the forefront of American industry to demonstrate their current thinking about the future, and continues the tradition of corporate participation in Tomorrowland. By doing so, Walt believed that he could get the public excited about all the wonders of technology that lie ahead.

Interior entertainment mural design by Mark Matuszak

BIBLIOGRAPHY

A Brush with Disney—An Artist's Journey, Told Through the Words and Works of Herbert Dickens Ryman, edited by Bruce Gordon and David Mumford, Camphor Tree Publishers, 2000

Designing Disney: Imagineering and the Art of the Show, John Hench with Peggy Van Pelt, Disney Editions, 2003

Designing Disney's Theme Parks: The Architecture of Reassurance, Karal Ann Marling, Flammarion/CCA, 1997

Disney: The First 100 Years, Dave Smith and Steven Clark, Hyperion, 1999, rev. 2002

Disney A to Z: The Official Encyclopedia, Dave Smith, Hyperion, 1996, rev. 1998, 2006

The Disney Mountains: Imagineering at Its Peak, Jason Surrell, Disney Editions, 2007

Disneyland, Martin A. Sklar, Walt Disney Productions, 1963

Disneyland: Dreams, Traditions and Transitions, Leonard Shannon, Disney's Kingdom Editions, 1994

Disneyland: The Inside Story, Randy Bright, Harry N. Abrams, Inc., 1987

Disneyland: The Nickel Tour, David Mumford and Bruce Gordon, Camphor Tree Publishers, 1995

The Haunted Mansion: From the Magic Kingdom to the Movies, Jason Surrell, Disney Editions, 2003

Pirates of the Caribbean: From the Magic Kingdom to the Movies, Jason Surrell, Disney Editions, 2005

Remembering Walt: Favorite Memories of Walt Disney, Amy Boothe Green and Howard E. Green, Disney Editions, 1999

Walt Disney, An American Original, Bob Thomas, Simon and Schuster, 1976; Hyperion 1994

Walt Disney Imagineering: A Behind the Dreams Look at Making the Magic Real, The Imagineers, Hyperion, 1996

Walt's Time: From Before to Beyond, Robert B. Sherman and Richard M. Sherman, Camphor Tree Publishers, 1998

Window on Main Street, Van Arsdale France, Stabur, 1991

We hope you've enjoyed this tour of Disneyland as much as we have. Now you can see the Park through the eyes of an Imagineer. Look for these and so many other little gems hidden in plain sight all throughout the Park. Have fun following in Walt's footsteps. But most of all, we hope you . . .

Enjoy the Park!